Remembering

HOME

Coming Home Series

J.M. ADELE

His plans just changed . . .
It was time to stop hiding behind his lens.

REMEMBERING HOME
Copyright © 2015 by J.M. Adele
All Rights Reserved

Edited by Eeva Lancaster
Cover Design by J.M. Adele
Cover Photo from Adobe Stock © Elena Kratovich
Cover art from brusheezy.com
Formatting by Book Flare Publishers

First Edition
ISBN: 978-0-9944516-5-1

*To all the authors who've gone before.
Thanks for being courageous and showing me
that it's possible.*

Contents

Chapter One

Self-hatred was the purest thing Aiden Thomas had felt in years. He stood in the bathroom of his hotel room, harsh, fluorescent light casting unforgiving shadows over the angles of his face. His shoulders wrenched up and down as each breath grew harder to drag in. The face reflected in the mirror twisted with shame and a fierce disgust. Black eyes bored into the mirror and back again in an infinite battle of wills and intimidation.

The news he'd discovered ten minutes ago was the baseball bat to the head he needed. A wakeup call after more than a decade of numb oblivion, isolation and ignorance. Aiden had let everyone down, including himself. He'd never see Hank Murphy again because he'd been behaving like a chicken shit, little boy. His teeth made a horrible grinding sound as he clenched his jaw.

The urge to destroy proved irresistible. He pounded his fist into the grim reflection, the shattering of the glass deafening in the small space. A satisfied smile crossed his face as he inspected his shredded knuckles. Aiden flexed his hand watching red spill down between his fingers, coloring the shards in the sink. It hurt like a bitch, and it felt fucking awesome.

The pussy in the mirror was gone. Aiden Thomas was awake and determined to make things right.

———

Almost a day later, he stood deliberately separate from a huddle of black sorrow, listening to the somber tones of a man of God eulogizing and offering prayer. A summary of the life of a man who meant so much to him, the one a young Aiden wished had been his real father.

The intermittent breeze carried away the murmurings of the minister, stirring the rich smell of freshly dug soil mixed with the more delicate scent of the floral adornment on the coffin. He sucked in the smells and the moisture in the southern air, grateful for some relief from the heaviness of his guilt. Beneath a makeshift bandage, his throbbing hand reminded him of the task ahead.

Aiden surveyed the crowd, recognizing most of his fellow mourners, although they were much older now. As a boy, he'd thought of them as his family until his father had disabused him of the notion, called him a foolish leech, and taught him that the only person he could truly rely on was himself.

He belonged to nobody.

All utter bullshit. He *had* belonged to Hank, his true father in every way that counted. He knew that now. Now that it was too late.

Jesus, Hank. I'm so sorry.

He set his jaw to prevent an agonized shout from escaping, as his eyes locked on the coffin. He forced them away, tilting his head side to side to loosen his neck. The pain from flexing his fingers allowed him to center his torment as far away from his heart as he could get it. It was welcome relief, however brief.

Aiden absorbed the poignant words, and looked around the gathering once again. A petite woman across from him drew his eyes. The only points of color were her red lips, and the green leaves and stem of a white rose visible through a curtain of raven hair. Each tear caught on the corner of her mouth before it trickled down her chin and fell to the earth. Her gloved hands clasped those of a fellow mourner's, obviously her close friend. They presented a striking contrast, a dark crown beside platinum blond. The women rocked slightly side-to-side, alternating between supporters and supported.

Something about the brunette pinched at his distant memories, imploring him to remember a familiarity long forgotten. Aiden's feet wanted to move of their own accord, to circle the huddle to get to her with some amount of stealth. He locked his knees refusing to bow to their demand, dropping his gaze to take in the grass beneath his feet. That'd be a good start. Embarrassing himself the first time he'd seen these people in fifteen years, and at the funeral of one of the town's most loved. His shoulders dropped as he pushed a long breath out, before raising his eyes once more.

The woman stood trembling, staring straight at him, barely holding it together. She was beyond beautiful, although agony etched her features. Her distressed state tugged at his protective side more than it should have, drawing the corners of his mouth down. Her big, doe-shaped eyes blinked through her tears, draining more rapidly now. Mouth quivering, her distress seemed to grow as she watched him. Jesus, she looked like she was going to collapse.

Aiden's right foot lifted and he stumbled forward slightly, catching himself before he could go any further. A prickle of awareness caused his stare to shift, taking in the narrowed gaze of her friend as she gripped onto her companion around the waist. He schooled his features, and quickly turned away. What the hell did he think he'd be able to do for her anyway?

Once again facing the Minister, he joined in the last prayers for his dear friend. "Rest in peace, old man," he said to himself, letting his grief wash over him once again. The minister finished the service and the coffin was lowered. A tepid breeze carried some dry leaves to join his friend in his final resting place in the ground.

Aiden watched as the woman broke away from her friend to throw a folded piece of paper and the rose onto the coffin. She made her way straight to him, stopping when the toes of their shoes tapped together, sending a jolt of adrenaline straight into his blood stream. He looked down at her leaning his shoulders away. *The fuck*? The closeness was jarring. Did she recognize him?

Her face tipped up, presenting him with her tear-stained beauty once more. Aiden pulled out a hanky from his jacket and offered it, needing to comfort her somehow.

"Thank y—" A sniffle and a gasp cut off her words. ". . . ou."

"Sorry for your loss." The rumble of his voice sounded deep as the inane words tumbled out of his mouth. He cringed inwardly. What could he say that didn't sound trite? *Hank would know what to say.*

Aiden's brown eyes drilled into her vivid green ones. She was an ethereal beauty. It was heartbreaking to witness the sadness pouring out of such perfection. Her head bobbed as she curled an unsteady hand around her throat, and burst into sobs.

"Oh sh—" He grimaced, raising a cautious hand to pat her on the shoulder. In response, she stepped into his side, grabbing onto the lapel of his jacket. Her jerky movements sent shock waves racing through his veins, the weight of her grip seeping into his bones. His mind blanked for a minute as his body took over. He shook his head to set his synapses scrambling, trying to make sense of this bizarre interaction.

When he arrived this morning, it sure didn't equate to a feeling of homecoming. He shouldn't have been surprised at the feeling of displacement and disconnection. That shit was pretty standard. But, this was Alabama. Where he grew up. The only place that had ever felt like home. Now? Sweet home Alabama? Not so much. Standing with his arm around this stranger . . . this felt more like home. Aiden's eyes almost crossed from system overload. His body hadn't really *felt* anything in so long. He was used to living the life of an international nomad, roaming between photo shoots. His only interactions with others coming from behind a camera lens.

What the hell is happening?

The woman's shudders slowly lessened to the softer, rise and fall of her chest, as she breathed deeply in acceptance of his comfort. *Huh.* He had been able to offer something after all. It speared his soul, connecting him to another in a way he had forgotten existed. His breathing slowed in time with hers, every inhale drawing her delicate, jasmine perfume, and the scent of salty tears. Aiden was drawing as much comfort as he was giving, the exchange probably weighing more heavily in his favor. In a moment of tortured surrender, this petite woman had made him see how lonely he was.

Loneliness was his MO.

His life sucked.

Goddamn.

It made him want to wrap himself around this woman, and never let go.

Their cocoon of comfort was shattered as she yanked her body away from his, crossing her arms, consternation written all over her face. At a loss for what to do, he shoved his hands in his pockets. Aiden dimly registered the sounds of car engines starting as the mourners lined up to leave, and the whispers of those few who remained.

"Are you coming to the wake?" Her eyes were almost pleading.

"Yes," his mouth spoke without connecting to his brain. His intention had been to pay his respects and leave, unsure if he'd even be welcome. Actually, he was certain he was unwelcome. Why was she asking him, a stranger?

Her head jerked in approval, before she again burrowed in the envelope of her friend's arms, the women then marched away. Aiden hadn't even noticed the blond move toward them. He'd been blissfully oblivious, completely absorbed by a woman for the first time in . . . forever.

He stood on liquid legs, elbows loose, missing the feel of her. Bewilderment doused his ability to think, as he watched her retreat. Something about the texture of her movement stirred the familiarity again. His memories rose closer to the surface, but faded again as she disappeared out of sight.

The energy in the air was noticeably different. Heaviness descended over him again as he turned to the grave to add a shovelful of dirt. Three other men remained to do the same.

"It's good to see ye again, Aiden. Sorry it couldn't have been under happier circumstances." Harry, his friend's brother, gave him a slap on the shoulder in greeting. The sentiment confused and chipped at his expectation to be treated like a stranger.

He paused to collect his wits, gathering the appropriate words from unused corners of his brain. "I'm crushed that I didn't get to see him again. He was more of a father to me than my own." The truth came rushing out, striking him straight through the heart. "I'm so sorry for your loss." He addressed all three men, again frustrated that he couldn't think of anything better to say. Harry's younger brother, Harvey, and Mr. Saunders, the neighbor from across the street, joined Harry.

Hank had been the oldest brother. A tall and sturdy Irishman with masses of black hair, and a beard to match. The younger brothers had inherited red hair from their mother, but they all had the same goliath stature.

In comical contrast, Mr. Saunders was a petite man with thin white wisps of hair. His eyebrows and eyelashes almost invisible against his pale pink skin.

All three men were in their sixties now. Patches of white had bleached the red hair at the brothers' temples, with several strays flecked about, elsewhere. It was shocking, how much they had aged. He supposed they could say the same about him. He was not yet sixteen when his parents moved him north.

"Would ye like a lift to the wake, then?" Harry asked.

"I don't suppose ye've got a car, at the minute?" Harvey threw a heavy arm around Aiden's shoulder, stretching slightly, as they were the same height.

"That'd be great, thanks."

Harry and Mr. Saunders took a more luxurious, Buick, while Harvey promptly guided Aiden to a rusty, old, Chevy pick-up. He knew that it used to be candy apple red. The painted logo of Harvey's Auto Shop had faded from the hood over time.

The slamming of their doors was loud, but the rumble of the engine was deafening. His shoes slipped and crunched on the collection of empty chip packets and coffee cups strewn on the floor of the passenger side. Harvey looked over to investigate, propping his sunglasses on his nose. "Sorry 'bout the mess. I needed sustenance to get me through the long hospital waits. Just kick it out of the way." He waved his hand as if brushing the offending items away, stirring the smell of sweat and stale coffee.

Aiden took in the scenery as the old truck bumped along; its shock absorbers not up to the task. The town had changed in his absence. Grassy fields had made way for new housing developments. The single traffic light had spawned some friends, though the center of town had mostly remained in its time capsule.

Aiden's knee jiggled against the door as his nervous energy found an outlet. He was still reeling from the weirdest moment of his life. Seeing his friend put underground, and experiencing what felt like salvation all within moments of each other. He had to put *her* out of his mind and focus on Hank.

"How long was he ill?"

"Oh, he had the first stroke about a month ago. It wasn't too bad. He could still talk, though his words were slurred. We thought he'd recover. He was starting rehab, but then he had a massive stroke. Turned him into a vegetable. No coming back from that. He was in a coma for a week before he died. Nasty business, seeing a strong, proud man brought to his knees. Even more horrible, seeing a brother suffer."

Aiden kept a steady eye on the road, using the horizon to ground him, and stop the flow of tears that threatened. He swallowed against a tight throat before attempting to speak. "I didn't know." He cursed under his breath. "I would have come." *I should have been here.*

"I just happened to look up the local paper online. I don't even know what made me do it. His name caught my eye while I was skimming." Aiden swallowed again, and turned to the window to squeeze his eyes shut.

He felt a firm grip on his shoulder. "Per'aps you wanted news of a certain young lady, as well as her pa?"

Hank's daughter, Angel. If he weren't in the habit of denying his true desires, he'd admit that he'd been searching the group of mourners for her. The girl he would never forget no matter how hard he tried. Angel. An appropriate name for the girl who weaved through his thoughts whenever he let them drift.

He sucked in a breath. Light dawned, and memories of green eyes that used to be shadowed behind glasses rose abruptly into transparency. Climbing trees and fishing, later became holding hands and kissing.

Angel.

His plans just changed.

Chapter Two

Thoughts of her broke the fissure around his heart wide open. His mind transported back to the day he left. The day his heart bled for leaving her. Stupidly, he had been searching for the sixteen-year-old Angel, forgetting to make a concession for time's passing.

The Chevy made a high-pitched squealing sound as its brakes protested. The sound sliced through his brief reverie, snapping him back to reality. He was about to see those green eyes again. Even puffy, bloodshot and flooded with tears, they were phenomenal.

"Time to celebrate the large life of my brother," Harvey slapped Aiden on the leg, and cranked the emergency brake. The noisy engine cut off, revealing a ringing in Aiden's ears.

Still reeling, Aiden blinked his eyes to focus on the old antebellum house. Behind him, cars lined both sides of the street under a canopy of oaks. The house was the same, although faded by time. The shutters were now a powder blue, rather than the original, deep, sky blue. Tall, white columns supported a portico proudly framing the double wooden doors. One of them stood open in welcome. The chatter of people beyond became louder as he neared.

His palms started to sweat, prompting him to lose the jacket. There was one person he was desperate to see on the other side of the threshold. The hammering of his blood pummeled his insides. The swing of emotions he was experiencing today was bound to leave bruises.

The onslaught only worsened when he entered the parlor to find Angel sitting in an elegant pose on a sofa. Her red lips and large eyes in stark, beautiful contrast to her pale skin. Hank's family and friends were milling about between the living areas, with drinks and plates of food. They all faded into the background when he saw Angel.

The waif of a girl had blossomed into a ravishing woman. Aiden was awestruck. She was a green-eyed, Audrey Hepburn lookalike. With curves, he noted, as his eyes lowered to the swells of her breasts pressed against her simple, black sheath dress. *Eyes above the neck, Thomas.* Christ, what a time to notice, but how could he not? Gone were the glasses and the braces. She had stopped dyeing her hair red to look like her cousins. Slender legs encased in stockings and black heels replaced the scraped knees and scuffed sneakers.

The boisterous tomboy was now all woman.

Her gaze honed in on him, a mix of emotions held suspended in one look. That was all it took to confirm what a coward and an idiot he had been. All that time lost, wandering, when paradise was here all along.

———

Angel's heels clicked on the checkerboard tile as she weaved between her mother's beloved antique furniture, and the friends and family who had come to celebrate her daddy's life. Stopping every now and then to make sure everybody had what they needed. She captured nostalgic retellings of his humor and generosity before the words drifted, gathering along the high ceilings, blanketing the room in love.

Another soft squeeze of reassurance on her shoulder was her cue to move on. With a sad smile, she wandered over to the pitcher of sweet tea. Angel gulped down the cool liquid, surveying the room, admiring how whitewashed wainscoting topped by powder blue wallpaper wrapped the room in class.

She moved to a window, her hand smoothing away the dust collected on a decorative pilaster. The view through the glass was obscured by an overgrown hedge. The parlor was a forbidden zone when she was a young girl covered head to toe in dirt. She'd stood at this window, nose pressed against the pane, hands cupped around her face to block the sunlight, admiring all the beauty that had accumulated over the generations.

With a weary sigh, Angel headed over to sit on a brocade sofa to await Aiden's arrival. Her pulsing nerves rendered her legs unsteady on the cursed heels. The seat was firm, built for posture rather than comfort. How her parents had liked a nightly cuddle on it, she'd never understand. But she wanted what they had all the same. In her youth, she thought she'd found *it*, but *it* was snatched away by a brute. She could think of other names to call him, but she'd never utter them aloud. Okay, she'd never utter them in company.

He'd better not dare to show his face at her daddy's wake. Angel's face screwed up in anger, her eyes blazing at the remnants of her sweet tea, but unseeing of their physical target.

Laughter and exclamations were the dominant sounds in the room. She let them fill her with pride and thankfulness for being Hank's daughter, erasing the stained memory from the past.

The last five weeks had been hard. Watching her daddy suffer had been excruciating. When he finally passed, it was an awful, unforgivable relief. She didn't want him to die, but she couldn't bear to see him suffering. A horrendous dilemma. Nothing could have prepared her for the experience of watching his coffin being lowered into the grave. The fact that his body was now an empty shell, shunted into reality before her eyes.

The pain of losing her father would always be a dull ache behind her breastbone. Loss seemed to be a theme in her life. First her mama, then Aiden, and now Daddy. But there's no way she'll let it get the better of her. Daddy would be disappointed if she didn't grab life with both hands and keep pushing through. She wasn't made that way, anyways. Angel was damn good at making lemonade. *Bring on the lemons and watch me juice those suckers.*

Aiden's back. If anything was going to test her lemonade making skills, this was it. Her speck of hope that he'd return had never perished, despite her malicious attempts to kill it. At first, she had twisted and mangled all her cherished memories of the boy she loved until, in her mind, he was a pitiful whimpering fool. Later, she had convinced herself that he had died. She hated that she had to do that to survive his loss. Finally, she conceded that he didn't love her enough to return.

All the speculations vanished the moment she had set eyes on him again. He was very much alive and no whimpering fool. *Lord, help me!* She didn't know whether to hug him or slap him. Apparently, she had chosen falling to pieces all over him. *Ugh.* She wanted to slap herself.

Angel's skin started to prickle, her muscles thrumming from an invisible pull. She spotted Aiden just inside the entrance to the parlor against the backdrop of the winding, grand staircase. The pull towards him had always been a tangible thing. It was unwelcome right now.

He looked so tall and handsome in his black slacks and white shirt. At the funeral, he had looked at her through a stranger's eyes. She registered the shock on his face now. It was obvious he had finally realized who she was.

Why did he have to come back now? She didn't know if her heart could take the added torment.

His trimmed, honey colored hair was a little longer on top so it fell across his forehead. He wiped his hands down the side of his pants as he approached. She noticed his right hand, wrapped in a bandage.

"Angel? I didn't recognize you before. I'm . . . sorry your daddy is gone." He paused to take a deep breath, his expression pained. "I'm s—" He gripped his jaw, pressing into his cheeks as if he was trying to push the words back in. "You've all been through hell." He bent to kiss her cheek. Instead of moving away, he folded himself into the space beside her and took her hand. "It's so good to see you again," he added, with sincerity and apparent relief as he expelled the words.

Was it really? Why did he wait so long to come back if he had missed her? How did he feel about being back here? She wanted to fire the questions at him like bullets, but the feel of his hand feeding a low hum of electricity into hers was distracting. *Stupid hand.*

Aiden's eyes roamed her face, taking in her transformation. "You've changed so much."

"So have you, but I still see the boy I used to know."

She couldn't resist reaching up to run her finger down the slight bend in his nose where it had been broken. His skin was warm and smooth. It felt so right to be in contact with it. The path of her touch continued across the scar on his cheekbone from a baseball incident years before. He made a sound as his breath caught, and she let her hand drop.

Angel sat compelled by his whiskey eyes, letting his spell weave an intricate net around her once more—just for a second. Variations of this exact moment had been in her dreams for years. Never did she imagine seeing him again under these circumstances. She couldn't deny her wish to be captured by him, but he had the worst timing known to man, and he wasn't here for her, anyways.

Seeing him at the funeral had nearly bowled her over. She had to touch him to know he was real, allowing his presence to ground her. The uncertainty surrounding his arrival meant it was more likely she would have to survive without it, as she had done for years. She'd done a damn good job of it, too.

"Daddy would have loved that you're finally back. He went a bit far in his efforts to get you here, though." Dark humor. She cringed at Aiden's expression, a mix of mortification and amusement, obviously struck dumb.

She was torn. So many questions weaved convoluted paths through her thoughts, confusing and frustrating her. "Why . . ." She shook her head and licked her lips. Nope. She couldn't do this here. "Would you like a drink, or somethin' to eat?"

Manners, she reminded herself. Mama was always on about manners. Advice that she had totally ignored until her sudden catapult into womanhood.

Aiden blinked, taking a moment to reply. "I'll get it. Do you want a refill?" He nodded towards the empty glass on the coffee table in front of them.

"Just some water. Thanks." She smiled and pulled her hands away, although a part of her was reluctant to let him go, she knew putting her guard up was necessary.

The smell of fried food churned her gut, mirroring her emotions. How much longer would she have to bear this? Her eyes darted around the room, scanning for an excuse to escape.

He watched her a beat longer, clearly perplexed. She knew she was being standoffish. *What did he expect? Lordy!*

"Aiden! C'mere and get some purdies," Harvey's voice boomed from the adjacent dining room. *Good ole' Uncle Harvey.*

Aiden's brow remained crinkled in confusion. "He means potatoes," Angel explained.

Understanding dawned on his face, and the smile that always made her melt, came out to play. "He hasn't changed a bit. If potatoes are purdies does that mean tomatoes are turdies?" An inelegant snort burst out before she could stop it. He was trying to defuse the awkwardness. She appreciated that.

Aiden's face split into a wide grin. "I'll be back. Don't go anywhere. We have a lot to catch up on."

"Mm hmm," she murmured to his retreating back. *More than you know.*

Chapter Three

He still moved the same. She had always loved the way he moved. Angel shook her head. It was no good letting her thoughts wander in *that* direction. He's not here to stay, only to pay his respects.

Angel's friend, Chelsea, dropped onto the sofa beside her, blond hair bouncing. "Don't go there." Her tone was stern, her eyes beseeching.

"No. I know. He's not stayin'," Angel's eyes dropped to watch the way she twisted her fingers together. "That's probably for the best." Her shoulders sank in defeat, and probably a little from relief. The situation was so complicated it gave her a headache.

"Are you gonna tell him?" Chelsea laid her hand on Angel's arm, a subtle prompt to stop her nervous twitching.

"He should know, but . . . I don't want him to feel—"

"Here you go." Angel's head popped up at the interruption. "One water, as requested." Aiden smiled at the two women, and placed the glass in front of Angel. He turned to Chelsea, holding out his hand. "Hi. I'm Aiden Thomas. I used to live down the road."

Angel frowned and her hands started twisting more violently. '*I used to live down the road*'. Not, '*Angel and I used to date*', or '*I used to love Angel, once*'. *Oh Lord, would ya listen to me.* Let the nit picking begin.

"Chelsea. Best friend and wing woman." She grabbed his bandaged hand firmly, and gave it one pump. Angel snorted at her friend's intimidation tactics. Chelsea tilted her head towards Angel, with an impish grin.

The most valuable friend is the one who can cheer you up when life turns to cow dung. She would forever be grateful to Chelsea's mama for deciding to move her teenage daughter away from Montgomery at a time when she needed her the most.

"What did ya do to your hand?"

"Oh." He flipped his hand over, carefully spreading his fingers. "I had a disagreement with a mirror."

"*Hmm.*" Chelsea's lips puckered, her eyebrows raised. "So, where do you live now?" Typical Chelsea, she wasn't wasting any time getting to the point.

Aiden sat in a wingback chair opposite Angel, and placed his own glass down. He didn't use a coaster. She had to bite her tongue. *Pick, pick.*

"I don't really have a home base. I live out of my suitcase." Angel reached for her water. She needed to wet her parched throat and occupy her hands. Fidgeting was so unladylike, her mama had told her a thousand times.

"That could get old real quick."

"I never thought so, until very recently." His eyes flickered over to Angel. She bit her lips to stop herself from speaking. She might say something stupid. Lack of a verbal filter was Chelsea's deal, not Angel's.

"What are ya doin' all that travelling for, anyways?" Chelsea was frowning at him as if he was stupid.

"I'm a freelance photographer. I go where the work is. I have several publications that request for my services, so I end up all over the place."

"Ooh, you've hit the bigtime. I guess you would never live in a Podunk place like this?" Chelsea peeked at Angel out of the corner of her eye.

"I loved growing up here. Never wanted to leave, actually." Aiden's intense gaze travelled over Angel's face. A warm blush trailed in its path, across her cheeks, and down her neck. Her nipples pebbled, awakening. As far as her body was concerned, Aiden Thomas was irresistible, and she had waited a long time to have him this close again. Not close enough. *Worst timing ever.*

Angel stared at him intently, searching for signs of truth in his statement. She used to be able to read him so clearly. She swallowed the bitter realization that he had changed. She didn't know him anymore. The Aiden she knew would never have punched a mirror. The Aiden she knew wasn't so . . . detached. Even his accent was different. The southern twang long erased. The thing was, he didn't know her either. Angel had lived a lifetime while he was tripping around the world.

She tuned back into the interrogation at the tail end of Chelsea's next question. ". . . you leave, then?"

"My parents moved us to Chicago for work. They're still there. I see them every now and then." The underlying strain in his voice making it clear that he'd rather poke a stick in his eye than visit his folks. Just the mention of his family formed an ice crystal trail down her spine. It seemed he'd managed to distance himself from them, but not break off completely. She sat up straight, wrapping her arms around her ribcage to protect herself against the foreboding infusing her bones. Chelsea sensed her distress and wrapped an arm around her shoulder.

He ran his thumb over his eyebrow, taking the break in questioning as an opportunity to address Angel with one of his own. "Do you still live here?" He sounded incredulous. She bristled at his rudeness. *Well, he's still good at putting his foot in his mouth.*

His eyes widened, and he slapped his hand across his eyes. "No!" he groaned. "That's not what I meant. I meant, I'm glad you're here. I know you love it here. You're probably happily married with kids." His eyes dropped to her bare ring finger.

"Not married," she croaked. Suddenly she felt like she'd wasted her life, holed up in Nowhere Alabama.

No. She shook her head in denial. She hadn't been wasting her time. She had been doing important things, and she loved being near her family. They had saved her sanity when Aiden left.

"Are you happy?" he asked tentatively.

Tears welled in her eyes, and she started wringing her hands again. She had been happy before her father became ill.

"Oh, very smooth. Way to go, Douche." Chelsea popped up and jammed her hands on her hips. "Now you made her feel sorry for herself, days after losing her father. You'd better apologize, or I'll have to kick your ass."

"Chelsea," Angel admonished, sending her friend a look that said, *'Please do not cause a scene at my daddy's wake'.*

"What? He's eatin' his boot right now." Her southern twang getting more pronounced as her ire rose.

Aiden gripped his cheeks and chin in one hand, pulling them down before dropping his hands to rub across his knees. "I am sorry. More than you know. I don't know anything about what you've been through, but I'd like to find out. How you've been. What's happening in your life. What you want for the future. Could we . . ." He blew out a harsh breath. "I know this isn't the right time, but would you like to visit with me, soon? Whenever you're ready?"

Her heart sped up at the look of hope and desperation on his face. She needed to settle down. He didn't mean it *that* way. Her emotions were so close to tipping her off the ledge, she couldn't see straight. She didn't know if this was a good idea at all. He was drawing her in again, eroding her bravado and stepping over the line she had drawn between them. She didn't want to blow her life apart, only to have him leave again.

Angel squeezed her eyes shut. What am I thinking? He wasn't asking for forever. He was asking for one visit before he leaves again. She could survive through a couple of hours. Right?

"They're converting the old Thompson place into a B and B, but it's not open yet. Are you stayin' above the hardware store?" She blinked up at him.

"I was hoping to ask Mr. Saunders. That is, if he still owns the place."

"He does," she affirmed with a nod.

"Good to know some things never change." His gaze seemed to search for some answer from her. "Can I get your number and let you know where I'll be?" He stood up to retrieve his cell from his pocket.

"You can ring here at the house. The number hasn't changed in fifteen years." An unintentional sliver of bitterness cut at her tone. She had let that go a long time ago, but something inside her wanted to make him suffer just a little, for breaking his promise and not coming back for her.

He scratched his cheek. "I never needed to know the number when I was a kid because I practically lived here."

"So, look it up," she blurted, losing her control. She immediately bit her lips, and tucked her chin down.

Chelsea rolled her eyes. "Oh, for God's sakes! Talk about it tomorrow when I'm not within earshot." She rattled off the number for him, and he diligently added it into his contacts. "Did y'all used to fight when you were kids?"

"Yeah," they said in unison, making each other laugh and draining the tension.

"Okay." Aiden returned his phone to his pocket and picked up his untouched drink. "I'd better go and find Mr. S. Talk to you later?" He bent to kiss Angel on the cheek. She took a deep, quiet breath in. He wore cologne, but underneath was pure

Aiden. His woodsy smell burrowed into her buried memories. Good and bad. The kiss lingered on her cheek even after the contact was broken.

Aiden leaned down to shake Chelsea's hand again. "Lovely to meet you, Chelsea."

"Oh, for sure. Things are gonna get interesting 'round here. You best mind me." Chelsea's handshake was overzealous at best, her eyes fierce.

"Mmm." Aiden's head reared back. "I think you're under the impression that I'm going to hurt Angel. You obviously know how we parted ways. While I think it's none of your business, I can see that you're very close, and Angel respects you a lot. I just hope that you return the favor, and let her make her own decisions about the company she keeps." Aiden detached Chelsea's grip, and flexed his hand as he walked away to find Mr. Saunders.

Chelsea watched him walk away. "I think the boy has finally grown up. Damn, I've gotta admire anyone who can put me in my place."

Angel's shoulders trembled with her quiet laughter. "You're like my own personal guard dog."

"That's part of the job description." Chelsea collected Angel's left hand in both of hers. "Are you okay, hun?"

Angel fixed her eyes on the glass of water in front of her, reaching out to take a few gulps. As she lowered the glass, the water rippled from her tremors. She used her other hand to steady the drink before placing it back down. The adrenaline hit was going to fade soon and when it did, she'd better be near a soft horizontal surface.

The room vibrated with the low hum of conversation and laughter. Her father's family and friends celebrating a glorious life cut short. The vaporous dance of perfume and food odors continued, making her nauseous. Her skin was even more alabaster than normal. Her mind was reeling from recent events. She needed to retreat.

"No, not really. I'm going to lie down. Would you give my apologies?"

"Sure thing, hun. Take all the time you need." They stood and embraced. Angel grabbed her glass, and headed for the grand staircase. The smooth, wooden balustrade comforted and anchored her.

Coming home from the hospital and walking into the empty house for the first time after her daddy had died was eerie. She was the one who had to make all the decisions now. She was responsible for everything that happens under this roof. Her uncles and aunts were great, more than great, but they wouldn't be here during the dark, lonely hours. She had no parent to fall back on, no wise brain to pick, no strong shoulder to lean on. She was it. Full stop. Angel felt painfully adrift. Her thoughts returned to Aiden, wishing he could be here to carry some of the burden of grief.

She wanted to squash the flicker of hope she felt at seeing him again. Her life was great. She was happy. He would leave and things would return to normal. She huffed and shook her head as she stood in the doorway of her room. Music was blaring from a room two doors down. Normal. Uh huh. What's that again?

Chapter Four

"There ye are," Harvey bellowed. The Irish brothers crowded around the large dining table, holding their packed plates. "Come and grab a plate. Have some casserole, ye look too skinny." Harvey poked Aiden in the side. He jerked in response. "Just as I suspected. I can feel yer bones. Too much trekkin' around snapping pictures."

Rubbing his sore ribs, Aiden's eyebrows shot up in surprise. "How did you know I was a photographer?"

"Oh, Hank kept an eye on ye from afar. Got scrapbooks filled with clippings of yer photos from magazines and the like. Fancy stuff. Ye got talent, Lad." Harry joined in on the conversation while grabbing a second, maybe third, helping of Buffalo wings.

His mouth parted and the guilt intensified. He wanted to yell at his younger self to be stronger and fight against the control of his parents. Why didn't he fight for those he loved? There was no excusing his abandonment once he had found his own way. The loneliness wrapping around his heart was his own doing and he despised himself for it.

"Not to worry, Lad. He loved ye like a son. He knew ye had to find yer own way out from yer parents' rule."

Aiden squeezed his eyes shut and flared his nostrils, dragging in as much air as possible through his tightening throat.

Harvey draped his arm around Aiden's shoulders and squeezed. "Breathe lad. What's important is that y'are here now. If ye ask me, he was the one that guided ye back. It's grand altogether." Harvey looked left and right over his shoulders. "Where's Tim?"

"Right here," Mr. Saunders replied, approaching from the kitchen directly behind.

"Tim! Got some of the good stuff I see." Harvey bobbed his head at the glass of whiskey in Mr. Saunders' hand, his arm pulling on Aiden's neck.

"Aiden here is gonna need a place to stay. Ye mind him bunkin' at yers?" Harvey turned back to Aiden. "They're turnin' the old Thompson place into a bed and breakfast of sorts, but it's takin' a lifetime to get it done. Plagued by problems." Aiden jiggled as Harvey shook his head. "Ye could stay with me, but the rooms are all taken. I won't be the one to kick a young woman out of her room." Harry snorted before sucking the meat off another chicken bone. "Unless ye want to sleep on the sofa? Thought ye might need the space for yer chat with the lass."

"How did you—?"

Harvey barked out a laugh. "Logic, Lad. Logic. There's unfinished business there. Got to be sorted." He gave him a whack on the back and took his arm away, much to Aiden's relief. Harvey's arm was like a tree trunk. He pushed his shoulders back, attempting to reverse the strain.

Tim Saunders held out a key for him. "You remember the side doorway?"

Aiden nodded, taking the key. "Thank you, and Mr. Saunders? I owe you an extremely late apology for—"

"Don't worry about it, Son. It's all in the past. I'll be chargin' you rent this time, and you need to call me Tim or I'll feel old." The man's smile made him look like a mischievous elf.

He didn't deserve the kindness and acceptance he was receiving from these men. He wasn't fool enough to think Angel would be as accommodating.

He stayed another couple of hours, talking to Harvey and Harry's wives and their five redheaded daughters. A hum began in his chest and spread through his blood. A feeling he hadn't had since he was a kid. Belonging. Love.

Family.

His father had ripped it all away deliberately, out of jealousy and a misguided attempt at parenting. The Murphy family were bad news, in his parents' eyes. They saw his infatuation with Angel and couldn't accept it. He was broken for a long time.

Aiden thought he was over it. He realized now he had only hidden his pain. Buried it under a huge workload, and a feigned aversion to settling down. For the first time in fifteen years, he could feel what had been missing and he knew what he needed. He wasn't so confident that he'd get it.

———

Loose bits of bitumen crunched under his shoes in the alleyway beside Saunders' Hardware Store. It was a two-story brick building, built in the fifties. His photographer's eye could see the beauty in its rustic façade. He unlocked the scarred wooden door to the apartment above. It opened to a narrow stairway leading straight up, smelling musty from the damp air and disuse. He switched the light on. The pop and flash of the globe blowing cut through the air. He grabbed his cell, using the flashlight app to light his way.

Another door at the top marked the entry to the apartment. The hinges groaned as he pushed it open into the studio style apartment. To his left, windows lined the front wall, all covered with heavy blinds, letting in the barest hint of twilight around the edges. After placing his bags on the floor, he moved through the apartment towards the windows, lighting a narrow path with his phone.

Once all the blinds were raised, stirring up great puffs of dust, he slid open the creaky old windows for some much needed air. With shafts of dying light blanketing the room, a flood of memories struck him. The most exquisite and painful memories of his life. He had spent his last night in Alabama, in this room, as a fifteen-year-old runaway.

The back of the apartment housed a small kitchen in the corner to the right of the entry. In the far corner stood an enclosed bathroom with barely enough room for one person to stand. Behind that back wall was Mr. Saunders' storeroom.

Aiden remembered trying to be quiet on his night as a stowaway, when he heard Tim rummaging around for supplies.

The orange foldout sofa sat in the living area, with its back to the entrance. At least Tim had bought a flat screen since he was here last. It looked displaced in time against the brown exposed brick wall. The small dining table to the left of the entry had a view overlooking the street. Everything was either brown or orange in a shout out to the seventies.

It was old, but it was comfortable. He'd stayed in worse accommodations in some of the more remote locations he'd worked in.

Aiden made sure to turn the fridge on and load up the supplies he'd bought on the way. His stomach had exhausted its load of southern food from the wake, and was now calling out for a refill. The thought of sitting down to eat by himself didn't appeal. It just amplified his loneliness.

The last time he was in this room, Angel was with him. Now she was missing. She'd been lost to him since that time, and he'd tried to block out the feeling. Aiden looked around the room, remembering everything she'd said, everything they'd done the last time they saw each other. How bliss had morphed into torment. The way she'd screamed out his name, and sobbed as his father yanked him down the stairs. His body shuddered, thinking it was all going to happen again.

He didn't want to be here. He wanted to go back to where she was. Tomorrow was too goddamn far away. As he ate, he made the decision to call Angel before going to sleep, wanting to hear her voice and make certain she'd meet with him. The anticipation of seeing her again was equal parts nerve-wracking and thrilling.

She'd gone through hell today. He'd have to wait. He knew how to be patient when it counted.

———

No answer. No answer last night, no answer this morning. Sweat beaded on Aiden's skin as he hiked through the thick greenery clinging to the river's edge, the branches scratching on his exposed arms and legs. The camera bag on his back held some serious glass, though he'd left most of it back at the apartment. He was doing what he always did to escape from himself and his thoughts, but today it wasn't working. Maybe he wasn't as patient as he thought. Waiting for the perfect shot was easy, compared to waiting for the perfect woman. With both hands cradling the camera strapped around his neck, he managed to snap one last shot of a Chipping Sparrow with its rusty red cap, before packing up and heading back.

One of the first pictures he'd taken had been of a sparrow in Hank's yard. It was a total fluke of perfect timing. He'd received a hearty slap on the back after he'd showed it to Hank. The memory buzzed his heart with warmth and pain. Aiden swallowed past a lump in his throat. That man had given him his two greatest loves, and he'd never forget it. He wanted to honor him somehow. Maybe Harvey was right. Maybe Hank had guided him back to where he belonged. A second chance to make things right.

He pushed his feet faster, feeling an inexplicable urgency. Every step closer to town, closer to Angel, brought him more peace than anything else could. Now that he'd seen her, he was desperate to see her again. Des-per-ate. He admitted it. If he knew she felt the same, he'd be the happiest man alive.

Manic Monday had taken over sedate Sunday in the center of town. People buzzed in and out of businesses, running their errands. Aiden held his breath as an old clunker sputtered past, leaving a trail of exhaust fumes behind. A bunch of teens rode by on bikes and scooters, narrowly missing him, their raucous conversation unimpeded by their exertions.

He glanced across the street, his eyes drawn to the sway of dark tresses as a woman exited a coffee shop. She walked in the opposite direction, the material of her skirt swishing in time with her hair. He didn't need to see her face to know who she was.

With a cursory glance at the traffic, he sprinted to the other side. "Angel!" He watched her slim legs falter, her body turning while twisting on the balls of her feet. She held a tray with four cups of coffee, green eyes wide with alarm as she took in the sight of him. Stopping a few feet away, aware that he was sweaty, he gave her a wary smile. "Hi."

"Aiden—h-how are you?" Her gaze drifted over his face, down to his chest and arms, before snapping back to his eyes.

"Okay. More importantly, how are you?" He adjusted the weight of his pack, leaving his thumbs hooked under the straps on each side of his chest. Her eyes drifted down again. "Angel?"

"Hmm?" She tilted her face back up, eyebrows raised.

His lips curved in triumph. He'd rattled her. He tipped his chin to the tray she was holding. "Afternoon coffee run?"

Her hair fell forward as she dropped her face to have a look for herself. "Um, yeah. I'd better get them to the guys before they get cold."

She twisted her body around, leaving him with an apologetic smile. His stomach dropped, fresh sweat breaking out on his brow for a completely new reason.

He fell into step beside her, not giving her the chance to get away. "Where are you off to?"

"The auto shop. I run the office there now." Her shoulders had hunched, her words coming out harried. His stomach dropped even further. His second chance was off to a bad start. He didn't want to chase her away. Harassing her wasn't the way to win her back.

Aiden stopped walking, dropping his arms to his sides. The distance between them stretched a few more feet before she checked behind her. Uncertainty bordering on panic colored her expression. She was going to chew her lips to bits if she continued like that. He painted a wide smile on his face, aiming to reassure her. "I'll see you later then?"

She took two more steps, her lips making a popping sound as she set them free. "Mm hmm. Later, Aiden." He wanted to suck her red, swollen lips into his mouth to see if she still tasted the same. She'd disappeared around a corner before that thought had a chance to finish.

Aiden wandered back to sit on a bench. He needed a plan of . . . not attack, but persuasion, maybe. Hunger pains from different origins disturbed his stomach and his senses. He sat on the bench ignoring his stomach, willing his body to calm down, and praying for the patience that he left behind in the hotel room with the shattered mirror.

Chapter Five

Angel crept up the staircase noticing the door at the top was ajar. She heard the low hum of the television, the flicker of its light bouncing off the stairwell walls.

After the encounter in the street, she'd gone home exhausted. Her afternoon nap had been fitful, a result of her inner turmoil at the impending discussion with Aiden. She had woken up with a headache, and the knowledge that if he went wandering around the town, talking to the townsfolk, he'd probably get a shock. After taking some painkillers, showering, and throwing her hair in a messy bun, she arrived at Saunders'.

This couldn't wait until tomorrow. She needed to be the one to tell him. In private. Now, with her trembling hand stretched out to open the creaky door, she questioned her wisdom.

Stepping over the threshold, she saw a strip of light from under the bathroom door caught on the shag pile, the sound of water pelting tiles muted behind the barrier.

He'd made up the sofa bed. Feeling less than comfortable about sharing that space with him during the difficult conversation to come, she opted for the hard dining chair instead. At least she could stare through the television. A few stray baked beans and a half-eaten piece of toast decorated a plate left abandoned on the table, along with an empty beer bottle. The smell actually stirred her appetite. Maybe the nap had done her good after all. More likely, it was the prospect of getting this long overdue discussion done with.

The last time she saw Aiden before he left, was in this room. Their last moment together. The beginning and the end. Sanity and despair.

Her eyes dropped to bore through the back of the sofa. Memories danced through her vision. Their awkward teenage limbs tangled. Desperate sweaty palms racing over heated, innocent flesh. She was sixteen, and so in love with Aiden. That day, they'd come home from school to find a moving truck almost fully loaded with the contents of his house. They had sprinted to her place, both of them pitching a conniption fit. His parents were moving him away. No warning, no time to prepare or say goodbye. They'd made the rash decision to escape together, jumping on their bikes, and riding into town. After stashing the bikes behind a dumpster in the alley, between the drug store and the butcher, Angel had distracted Mr. Saunders while Aiden snuck behind the counter to steal the keys to the top floor.

They thought they could bunker down for the night and figure out a plan of escape. She knew deep down, it was their last night together. Mr. Thomas is a formidable, intelligent man. He'd find them. No doubt. Aiden, ever the dreamer, thought they had a chance. She didn't want him to leave without being with him at least one time.

Hearing the steady stream of water from the shower, her mind conjured images of a grown up Aiden, wet—and soapy. She cursed her wayward thoughts. She needed to stay on task.

Night had fallen. The air was cooler and smelled of rain. The clicking of crickets were audible through the open windows. She wandered towards the front, peeking down at the main street. The blinking of lightning bugs, and a few tired old streetlights were the only source of light outside. Thanks to heavy cloud cover. Not a soul was about. Just her . . . and Aiden.

Angel made sure to shut the blinds on the front windows, and switch on the light in the kitchen before returning to the table. The blinds billowed in and out with every breath of breeze, making a sucking sound as the stale air escaped. The same way they had that night, when her life was shattered, her future changed by an unforeseen twist.

The sound of the shower cut off. Her palms started to sweat. Angel wiped them on her jeans, and crossed her arms across her chest. She had on her lucky T-shirt. Aiden had bought it for her when they went to a Tim McGraw concert. It was too big back then, now she filled it so it stretched across her breasts.

The bathroom door cracked open. She inhaled sharply. *Oh my.* Aiden stepped out surrounded by steam, a towel wrapped around his waist. He had rubbed the towel through his hair leaving it sticking out in all directions. A few stray rivulets of water traced the contours of his body, catching on a patch of chest hair and running down his firm stomach. She watched every single drop. *Praise Jesus.*

He froze upon seeing her. "Sorry," she whispered. "You left the door unlocked. Tim wouldn't be happy with you."

He blinked, owl eyed. "What are you doing here?"

"I thought we could talk tonight, but I can see you're . . . getting ready for bed. You must be tired. I'll—"

"No I'm not. Not tired, I mean. Glad you're here." His voice was scratchy. He attempted a smile, but it fell short when his eyes dropped to her T-shirt.

Aiden's face was a picture of desire, his lids heavy, beautiful lips parted. The muscles of his chest heaved with each breath. He stood still. One hand grasped the towel and the other hung limply at his side.

At that moment, she waivered. She didn't come for this. If he left tomorrow without the chance of return, she'd always wonder what it would be like to be with this man. What they could have together. After an awful few weeks, she needed something life affirming. Something to make her feel alive and connected with someone she loved. Sitting here seeing Aiden, *the man,* and realizing her feelings had never faded, she just wanted to be reckless. To have just one night with him before everything changes. Before he leaves again. She promised herself she would be truthful with him in the morning, but for now, she needed him. Only him.

Her gaze raked up his body to his eyes. Angel unfurled her arms and stood.

"Don't say a word." Her voice quivered from lust and fear. Fear that he might not want her as she wanted him.

He didn't speak, only stalked towards her, reaching to cup her face in his hands. His eyes searing as he lowered his lips to hers. She closed her eyes and reached her hands up to grasp his wrists. The feathery brush of his lips against hers sent divine tingles shooting through her body. It was always like this when they kissed. He set her heart alight, and branded her as his with every stroke of his touch.

His hands moved to the nape of her neck and travelled down her shoulders and arms. She grabbed onto his waist, knocking the towel loose. His kiss became bruising. He reached down grabbing her thighs, urging her to wrap them around him so he could carry her to the sofa. She was way ahead of him, jumping at the suggestion.

Their tongues were tasting, licking, remembering each other, while her hands learned the matured contours of his back and shoulders.

He knelt down on the mattress and dropped forward, bracing himself on one hand. The springs squeaked as Angel bounced, dropping her legs from his body. She looked down his exceptional body to see his erection jutting out proudly. He was magnificent. She wanted him *now*. Skin on skin.

Angel wrenched off her top and started fumbling with the button of her jeans. Aiden's hands covered hers "Let me," he growled. She flopped back on the pillow and grabbed onto the edge of the mattress above her head, lifting her hips when he slid her jeans down.

"Shoes," she managed to pant.

Leaving her jeans bunched around her calves he slipped her ballet flats off and tossed them behind him. She heard one hit the wall and bounce off.

Like she cared.

He pulled the jeans off the rest of the way, and sat back on his heels taking in the sight of her in her simple, pink, cotton bra and panties. The way he watched her, she felt like she was wearing French lace.

He bent his head and placed a kiss on her mound taking a deep breath. "I can smell your arousal. I bet you taste delicious."

Oh, fuck. Adult Aiden liked dirty talk. Her muscles clenched. Apparently, so did she.

She blushed furiously. The thought of him tasting her *there* sent her pulse rocketing, and her core throbbing in anticipation. She had never had a man do that to her. Sex had mostly been perfunctory in her experience. Well, except for the first few times all those years ago on this sofa bed. Those times she held in the vault of her heart.

Aiden curled his fingers in the sides of her underwear, his knuckles grazing down her legs as he removed her panties. A delicious heat trailed the motion. She was panting rapidly, but couldn't bring herself to be embarrassed.

Aiden slid his tongue along her inner thigh as he moved towards his target. She felt his hot breath on her before his tongue darted out to taste. Her hips shot up off the bed at the sensation. She couldn't stifle the moan. *Oh my God. This is what all the fuss is about.* A small part of her felt indignant at the fact that she had missed this all these years.

Aiden's head bobbed as his tongue and lips and teeth worked their magic. His hands were holding her thighs down keeping her rocking to a minimum. The way his stubble worked her flesh into a frenzy had her shaking uncontrollably. Her fingers threaded through his damp hair pulling him closer.

The sight of him, his shoulders bunched, his dark eyes locked on hers and the feel of his hot tongue on her center, set her over the edge. Heat burst from her core and spread in pulsing waves. She cried out, bracing her tummy muscles and throwing her head back, fingers tugging at his hair.

He kept licking her, allowing her to come down slowly before kissing the soft flesh around her navel and up to the swells of her breasts above her bra.

She looked down noticing she was white knuckling clumps of his hair. Angel let go, mortified that she had been yanking it so hard.

He laughed at the expression on her face. "It's okay, I'm not bald yet."

She did an embarrassingly high-pitched giggle.

He pressed a kiss on her breastbone, moving his hands under her back to remove her bra. The cool breeze from the window rushed over her heated flesh. Aiden's eyes grew even darker at the sight of the soft, generous, swells, peaked with pale pink nipples. He sucked one hard point into his mouth, shooting tingles straight between her legs. He moved his hand, gently squeezing and massaging her breast as he sucked. His fingers continued working her nipple as he moved to suck the other side.

It was incredible. She was clutching on to his shoulders as if her life depended on it. On him.

Her legs wrapped around his back pulling him closer. "Aiden," she breathed his name, her vocal chords no longer functional.

He lurched up crashing his mouth down on hers in a branding kiss before leaving her.

She squeaked in protest.

"Relax, sweetheart. I have to get a condom."

Her shoulders sank back into the bed. He carried condoms in his wallet. Of course he did, he was an attractive single man. She had condoms in her bedside table so she couldn't judge, even if they were probably out of date.

Angel watched him pull out his wallet, grabbing the little packet. His cock bounced as he headed back to her. He stood beside the bed, ripping the packet open.

She sat up and wrapped her hand around his hard flesh. It pulsed under her touch. She felt a bit smug that she'd done this to him. Angel leaned forward, kissing the drop of moisture from the tip before running her tongue around the sensitive head, wanting to give him as much pleasure as he'd just given her. Aiden groaned. "You better stop that. I'm already close to blowing just looking at you and having your taste on my tongue."

She pulled back. He may as well have lit a match. She was on fire with want for him. "Hurry."

Aiden rolled the condom on quickly and dove onto the bed, pushing her back down. Angel pulled his hips into hers, guiding him to her throbbing core. Their groans of satisfaction filled the air as he slid slowly to the hilt. He stayed there for a couple of seconds, and she savored the full feeling before he started to glide his hips back, his hardness dragging against her slick flesh.

Incredible. She felt complete. She knew she shouldn't let her heart get involved again, but it was impossible because she'd never stopped loving him. He was her home, as much as this place and her family were. Something vital was always missing when he was gone.

Their bodies collided and drove each other to ecstasy. She grabbed two hands full of his firm ass, urging him deeper. His hips slammed into hers, the sound drowning out the squeaking bed. If anyone happened to be out on the street, there'd be no mistaking the noises coming from the windows above the hardware store. The thought drove her excitement even higher. She wasn't going to analyze whether she should be ashamed of that right now.

He moved his thumb between them to her still sensitive clit, adding just the right amount of pressure, sending her into bliss once again. Aiden grunted his satisfaction, the rhythm of his movements becoming jerky as he reached his peak, growling with pleasure. He collapsed on top of her, resting his face on the pillow beside her, leaning his weight on one shoulder. His harsh breathing loud in her ear, even though muffled.

Tears streamed down Angel's face without her knowing. Her frazzled emotions gaining hold again, as the fleeting bliss receded. She wanted to grab onto him once more, and lock him inside her. This was one of the best moments of her life, a glimpse into what could be. But she couldn't trust that it meant as much to him as it did to her. The doubt was a bucket of sand smothering the fire he'd sparked.

Losing her mother when she was a little girl had brought on nightmares for months, leaving her feeling vulnerable. Aiden leaving had nearly severed her in half, inciting the hardest time of her life. If he left again, she would have to pick herself up and get the best out of life somehow. She was a strong woman. She could survive without him.

He eased away and rolled off the bed, heading to the bathroom to discard the condom. She sat up, wiping her cheeks, frantically searching for her underwear. Darting off the bed, she yanked her panties on and found her bra on the coffee table, off to the side.

Aiden came back while she was unsuccessfully trying to hook it back up. "Hey, where're you going?" Panic dominated his voice.

"I . . . this wasn't meant to happen." She kept struggling with the clasp, in vain. The frustration brought on a fresh round of tears.

"Hey. Hey, it's okay." Aiden cocooned her in his arms and she went limp, letting all her pain and anger drain into him. He just took it, like he used to. He used to make everything better, just by being there.

When her tears subsided, she saw that he was still naked, and she'd made a snotty, wet mess on his shoulder.

"Oh, darn. Sorry. I'll go get your towel." He shook his head, and lowered her to sit on the edge of the bed.

"I couldn't give a fuck. Don't move," he ordered. He left her to get some tissues. Wiping her face with such tenderness when he returned, the waterworks threatened to start again.

He climbed onto the bed behind her, and pulled her down beside him, flicking her bra away and covering their bodies with the sheet.

"Talk to me." His breath fanned her neck making her shiver.

Angel stared through the open bathroom door. Steam swirled in beautiful patterns through the trail of light. Clearly, it hadn't taken them that long to get down to business.

Only fifteen years or so.

She closed her eyes and inhaled some courage. *Just say what you're thinking, it avoids so much crap later on.*

"I can't regret being with you. I've been waiting a long time and I needed—that—now more than ever. But you're not staying. We can't start something if we're not going to finish it. I know I'd survive it, but I don't want the agony again." As the words spilled out, she feared it might already be too late for that.

Angel opened her eyes and rolled to her back. She trained her gaze on the ceiling. No way was she going to look at him, and see regret in his eyes.

Aiden's arm circled her rib cage, and dragged her closer. He propped his leg across both of hers. His body heat was stoked to furnace level, a welcome thing considering she had gone cold at the thought of losing him. He was growing hard already against her thigh. Good to know he was as affected by her nearness as she was by his spectacular, naked form, pressed up against her.

"I don't plan on going anywhere. I have some details to sort out, but when I saw you again . . . I realized I haven't felt at home since I left you." He leaned in to kiss her neck. She wanted to whimper when he stopped. "Would it be so bad if I moved back?"

His voice sounded a little wounded. Did he think she didn't want him to stay?

Did she trust him to stay?

She wanted it more than she wanted to breathe. "It wouldn't be bad." She winced. It might be bad when he finds out. Reality was always there loitering behind the walls of her family home.

Angel had never had trouble expressing things. Bad news, good news, strong opinions. The outcome had never been this important before. Nerves corroded her stomach, not knowing how he was going to react when she told him about the sh— dung storm he'd left her to endure.

She hitched her legs over the side of the bed and threw the covers off. Aiden's limbs slid off her body, bouncing on the mattress from the speed of her retreat. Snatching her bra off the floor, she managed to hook it together on the first go this time. *Thank you, Jesus.*

She dressed quickly, needing armor for the next part of the conversation. Standing to face a wary Aiden, she steeled herself for whatever might happen.

"What's going on, Angel? Where are you going?" He was sitting up now, leaning back on his hands, arms locked. The sheet gathered around his waist and one leg was exposed.

She ordered her eyes not to stray below his neck. "I have something to tell you. You might not like it, but it is what it is. The last time we were here, like this," she waved her hand back and forth over the bed, "you left a part of yourself behind. With me."

"I know I did. I left my heart with you."

Oh. Why did he have to go and say something like that? He was looking at her with such adoration, like he used to. She dropped her head to search the floor for something, *please God*, anything interesting.

"Um. No. Well, yes, okay, but that's not what I meant." *Just say it, for the love of . . .* "You got me pregnant. We didn't use protection because we didn't have any, and we were on the run and—" Her words cut off at the sound of his choking.

She snapped her head up to look at his face. He was pasty white, almost turning grey. *Shit!* She couldn't be here for this part. Her legs made the decision to run for her. She grabbed her pocket book on the way, slamming the door to the apartment behind her. The sound of her footsteps pounded down the stairs, keeping pace with her pulse. She threw the bottom door open, leaving it as wide and gaping as Aiden's mouth had been.

Stupid. Stupid. She knew this would happen. Adrenaline coursed through her body, setting her insides on spin cycle.

No. It was the right thing to do. To tell him, before he left.

Well, he knows now. Some of it at least.

Angel wondered if he'd stick around to find out the rest.

Chapter Six

His blood rushed like a flash flood, the sound in his ears deafening. His vision narrowed to a black tunnel with memories showing a movie reel on the walls; points of light going at warp speed. He found it hard to grasp any of them.

Pregnant? He had left her pregnant. She had to go through that without him. The self-loathing came back full force. He should have been in contact as soon as he could, but instead he'd let his father's poisonous words in. He did that, no one else.

The memories of their last time together pinged around, abruptly morphing into images of a baby he had never seen, and then they came to a screeching halt.

Did she have the baby? Did she keep it? Was the baby okay? No, not baby—teenager.

The disbelief and shock turned to awe. He was a father and he was . . . *happy* about it.

The images cleared, and he saw his future reflected with clarity. He couldn't think of another woman who he'd choose to be the mother of his child. Angel was his and he was hers. It had been that way since they were six years old, meeting on the seesaw. Even as a little boy he had felt the gravity of that moment, and grabbed onto the special light that shone from Angel, never wanting to let go.

He wanted to meet his child. Now. Aiden looked around, coming back into awareness. He stood up, feeling stiff. Determination tightened his brow as he looked around for his phone, wondering how long he'd been in a stupor. One o'clock in the morning. Aiden didn't have a clue what time Angel left. There was no chance she'd open the door to him in the dead of night. No way he'd get to meet his child even if he—she, wanted to meet him.

He mentally flipped through all the young people he'd seen at the wake yesterday, vaguely remembering Harry's grandchildren. Two boys and three girls, he'd counted as their mothers had pointed them all out. They were too young anyway. Harvey's daughters were in their early twenties, visiting on their summer break from college. There were at least a dozen other teens roaming around. Which one was his?

Sleep was a distant possibility now. His hand throbbed as he put on a new bandage, tossing the damp one in the trash. After using the bathroom and throwing on jeans and a shirt, he made himself a cup of coffee, and filled a bottle with water. He needed the fortification for the long walk to Angel's house on the edge of town. He'd plaster his ass to her doorstep and the periphery of her life, for as long as it took her to open up and let him in.

————

Aiden's cell vibrated in his pocket for the second time this morning. The name 'Sir' displayed on the caller ID. *Nope, not dealing with him today*. His father was hounding him because he hadn't checked in this week. He stowed the phone in his back jeans pocket, and stared at Angel's front door again, surprised he hadn't put a hole in it by now.

The sun had already been up for a couple of hours before the gnawing ache to know became too much for Aiden. Abandoning his post on the tire swing in the front yard, he went to the front door and knocked, vibrating with his curiosity. After two minutes, there was still no answer. He spun around to head out back, his momentum halting when he grabbed onto one of the great columns that held up the portico at the click of the lock. Finally.

The entryway revealed a beautiful young woman with wavy brown hair and freckled skin. Green eyes stared up at him impatiently. "Yes? Can I help you?"

He swallowed. "Is your mama home?"

"Probably." Her slender shoulders jerked with indifference.

He frowned, gripping the column tighter. "Could you find out for me please?"

"Why don't you go see for yourself? She lives on the other side of town." Her arm flicked out to her right, narrowly missing a collision with the door.

Not his daughter. Relaxing his grip on the column, he walked back to the door. "Is Angel—"

"Who's at the door, Jessica?" A raven-haired sprite popped her head around to get a sticky beak at him.

His eyes levered open, his mouth parched, and his heart pumped harder, trying to jump out of his chest to get to this pixie of a girl. She was Angel all over again, without the glasses and dyed red hair. Her eyes were more hazel than green.

"Hi." She waved at him with a big smile, so similar to her mother's it warmed his insides. "I guess you're my daddy, huh? 'Bout time ya got here." The tiny amount of breeze generated by that wave could've knocked him down for the count. He swayed on his less than sturdy legs. "You better come in. Mama said you might come over." The girls stepped aside to usher him in while his daughter—*his daughter*, yelled for her mother.

They went through to the kitchen, leaving him to sit at the table in the breakfast nook. Large windows framed the view of the lawn and gardens beyond. An outdoor setting sat off to the side of the large patio, partially hidden. Nature was making the most of the family's turmoil and neglect, overgrown grass and weeds thriving and choking the other plants.

The girls sat on high stools at the kitchen counter, his daughter wearing a smile, Jessica wearing a smirk.

"Can I ask your name?" He addressed his daughter.

She nodded. "Aidrena. Addy for short. It's my grandmother's name mixed with yours, if you didn't guess. "I've seen your photos. They're beautiful. Grandad kept some scrapbooks. Mama helped. We searched through the magazines we knew you worked for. Could never pin you down though. Where ya been?"

He hung on every word she said, desperately trying to keep up with the rapid subject changes. Watching her speak was surreal, he imagined somewhere in heaven, the angels were heralding a miracle with the release of each syllable from her mouth. "I've been everywhere, nowhere . . . You look so much like your mama." He had to say it. Couldn't get over it. "I had no idea. I—I would've found my way back if I'd known." *I wish I had known.*

"It's okay. You're here now. You stayin'?"

"Yeah." His reply was swift. He already knew it the second he'd seen Angel sitting on that ancient sofa. He wouldn't leave her again. He just needed to figure out what to do with his career and now, how to be a father.

"You came." Angel's awed voice drifted from the doorway.

He twisted to face her. Her beauty was astonishing. Even in a simple tank top and denim skirt and without makeup, she was loveliness personified. "Of course."

Her face was a picture of disbelief. She grimaced before straightening her features out. She never was good at poker face. He was a little hurt that she thought he wouldn't want to meet his child. Starting now, his mission was to prove to her that he wanted to be here. It was time to take back his future, and be where he belonged.

A crop of shaggy blond hair appeared behind Angel's head. "Mornin'," a deep voice mumbled. Angel stood to the side to let a gangly teen pass by. He wore boxer shorts and a threadbare T-shirt. His feet shuffled along the tile, his mouth wide in a yawn as he scrubbed the fatigue from his face.

"Mornin', Snickers!" Addy chirped.

How many friends was she having sleepover? And why is Angel allowing a *boy* to sleep over? He knew this wasn't a cousin. He didn't remember Jessica, but he remembered enough to know none of Harry or Harvey's grandkids had blonde hair. *Huh.* He guessed the fathering instinct wasn't that far under the surface.

The boy grunted at the greeting, and buried his head in the fridge, rearranging its contents to find his morning sustenance.

Aiden returned his attention to Angel. She was twisting her fingers together, biting her lip and darting her eyes from the boy obscured by the fridge door back to Aiden. The teen's tall frame backed away, letting the door snap shut. With orange juice dangling in one hand, a carton of eggs gripped in the other, and a slice of cheese wedged between his teeth, he turned to put his haul on the bench.

Aiden watched with fascination as the young man raised his head, taking in the fact they had a visitor. The boy looked familiar. He had the same mouth and nose as Angel, but the same brown eyes Aiden had seen in the mirror all his life. Hair the same color and texture as his own. A frame identical to his at the age of fourteen.

It was too much to process. Aiden's brain short-circuited. The pulse behind his temples rivalled the noise of a jet engine. Ant colonies had taken up residence under his skin. This boy was his. The young version of himself looked back at him with a blank expression.

Angel came up beside the teenager, and put her arm around his waist. "You've met Aidrena, our daughter." Angel nodded her head towards Addy. "This is Harrison, our son. Also known as Sonny," she added, clutching the boy closer to her side.

"Twins," he rasped, wiping his sweaty palms on his jeans. *Christ, poor Angel.*

Harrison slowly extended his hand towards his father. "Nice to meet you, sir." His voice was croaky, whether from sleep, typical teenage changes, or wariness, Aiden didn't know.

There was no way his son was going to call him Sir. Fueled by adrenaline, he surged forward a little too quickly to grasp his son's hand in both of his, just holding on in amazement. "Call me . . ." *Dad*, "Aiden." Harrison was quick to shake off the grip, not as accepting as his sister had been. He looked to his mother for guidance.

Angel let go of Harrison and clasped her hands, twisting her fingers enough to compromise the blood flow. "Aiden, come on out back and talk with me awhile," Angel offered, breaking into the awkwardness.

Aiden dragged his gaze away from the sight of his son and forced his feet to follow Angel. He wanted to get to know the miracles he had helped to create, but he knew it would take time for them all to readjust to the reality of him. He wanted to curse his father repeatedly.

He wanted to punch that mirror all over again.

————

Angel led Aiden outside, where they sat facing each other across the mosaic-topped table. Clumps of Hibiscus formed a line of bystanders on each side of the paved patio. The grass was knee high out here, she'd have to ask Harrison to mow it later on. The sounds of morning in early summer speckled the air.

The yard held her favorite memories, her personal time capsule of happiness. Time spent with all the people she loved in the world. Even when Mother Nature was pitching a hissy fit, Angel liked to sit and watch the show through the kitchen windows. The thrashing of wind through the tree branches, lit by electric flashes of light was always spectacular. She felt a bit like one of those storms was whipping up her insides.

Using her happy place as an anchor, she turned towards Aiden; watching, waiting, gauging his reaction to meeting their children. His brown eyes brimmed with emotion. "I won't ask why you didn't tell me. I know why. I feel like such a shit." Aiden dragged his palm down over his face, and rested his elbows on his knees, hanging his head.

He pulled his head back up slowly. His eyes steadied on hers, resolve solidified in his stare. "You told them about me." It wasn't a question, and his voice betrayed the depth of his thanks.

"I wanted them to know you in some small way. I wouldn't have them thinking they were abandoned." She scooped some hair behind her ear and blinked back at him, trying to order her thoughts.

Where the heck do I start?

She breathed deep and let the purge begin. "Why didn't you call? Or write? I had no way of reaching you. They dragged you away and you just . . . vanished." She waved her hand, stirring the earthy smell. Embarrassed that her voice had become so shrill, she cleared her throat, waiting for his response.

"I . . ." he huffed and rubbed his face vigorously before dropping his arms on his lap. "My father . . . he knew where I was every minute of the day. He wouldn't allow me to use the phone. He forbade any form of communication with the people of this town. I had no life outside of school and home. The hired help monitored my whereabouts. He grounded me as my punishment for running away. With you."

Aiden leaned down, placing his elbows back on his knees. "I don't want to give you a bunch of weak excuses. Truth is, I probably could have found a way to use a phone in school, but I never did. I was his pathetic puppet and prisoner. After a while, I just . . . gave up. You couldn't possibly hate me any more than I hate myself, right now."

The level of anger she held onto started to wane. She could just imagine Brenton Thomas doing that. She knew there was more to it than just prejudice against her and her family. There was so much Aiden still didn't understand. Her heart went out to the young man who was treated so badly.

She remembered him being an introspective soul. He would spend long moments inside his own head, just figuring out his views of the world. Angel used to watch him, wondering where his thoughts had taken him. He loved photography even back then. Her father had given Aiden a camera and kept his film supply stocked. They had a dark room set up for him. Aiden spent hours in there, bathed in a red hue, pegging up his artwork. The smell of the chemicals always reminded her of him. Not that she needed any more reminders.

Angel dragged her chair beside his, the grating, metallic sound breaking the tension only a little. "Later then. Why didn't you get in touch?"

Aiden leaned back in his chair, tipping his head back briefly to break eye contact, probably needing a reprieve. He focused on her once again. "By then, I didn't believe my immature memories of us, or this place. My father convinced me that you all felt sorry for a pathetic boy. I was insecure enough to buy it. He told me I was unlovable so many times. That sort of thing soaks into a child's mind like poison."

Oh, Aiden . . . That sonofabitch, Brenton. Yes, she was swearing. In her head. Her stomach rolled at the thought of his father's abuse. "I don't understand how you couldn't know, why you didn't believe we loved you. Did I not show it or say it enough?" Angel grabbed his hand, and placed it over her heart. "When you left, I broke in two," she whispered. Tears cascaded down her cheeks. Inside, she felt bone dry. How could there be more tears when she'd cried an ocean's worth in the last few weeks. She dropped his hand and leaned away. "I figured, maybe you'd try to return once you finished college, or maybe when you turned twenty one, but the years marched on by and still nothing. That . . ." Angel hiccupped, her shoulders jumping.

"Shit. Don't cry, please?" Expression pained, he reached for her hand again.

"I'm n-not fin-nished." Angel dragged the back of her hand across her cheeks while trying to regain her composure. "That was like a bullet wound that s-slowly drained me of b-blood. That drew out the agony of l-losing you." Her shoulders bunched up as she dragged in a breath. "I really thought I was okay, but seeing you has opened up the old wounds again."

He leaned over and wrapped his strong arms around her, tucking her under his chin. "I'm so, so sorry . . . for being weak and for not trusting in your love and your father's. Hell, your whole family's. They welcomed me back with open arms yesterday. It blew me away." He leaned back and cupped her cheeks in his palms. "I'm sorry. Please forgive me, Angel?"

Her gaze burrowed into his dark eyes, searching for a reflection of the emotions she was feeling. She saw something, but didn't trust it enough to label it. His thumbs wiped away her tears. Angel didn't dwell on how good it felt to be in his arms again . . . how right.

She nodded her head in acknowledgement of what he'd said. He would have to earn her forgiveness, and it wasn't going to be easy. "We'll see." She leaned away to look him in the eye. "How did you find out about Daddy?"

"Something told me to check online for the local paper. When I saw the funeral notice . . . uh, the shock . . . was the worst kind of pain, but it snapped me awake."

He moved a few stray strands of her hair to tuck them behind her ear. She shivered with the motion. He used to do that all the time. She bit her lips, looking down at her lap. The next question had to be asked. She steeled herself for possible disappointment when he answered.

"How . . ." her voice cracked. She cleared her throat to try again. "How long are you staying?"

She felt his hand stroke the back of her head and down the length of her hair. She wanted to purr. "I don't know." Her damp lashes brushed her cheeks as her eyelids dropped. At least he didn't say he was leaving right away. "I cancelled all my bookings, left everything on pause. A buddy of mine is storing some of my stuff at his place in New York. I'll need to sort out some things before I know when I'll be able to get back."

Yep, he was leaving, but with the possibility of return.

Breathe, just breathe.

She watched her fingers twist and squeeze. Her heart galloped behind her rib cage, never actually getting anywhere . . . much like her love for Aiden. It was worse now. To have a glimmer of hope that he might want to stay.

God, she hoped he *wanted* to stay.

Chapter Seven

"Well now, isn't that adorable." Chelsea's trademark snark greeted them.

Angel's head reared back, her body stiffening briefly, before recognition took over her features. "Mornin'." She contorted her face, unable to manage a smile.

Chelsea looked pretty in her white sundress, with her hair braided and her cowboy boots ready to stomp on the nearest person who said the wrong thing. "So, I guess this means y'all kissed and made up?" She stood with one hip out, both hands holding it as if she was scared it was going to dislocate. Her left eyebrow reached for the heavens, a smirk front and center.

Angel turned back to Aiden, an inscrutable look in place. "I wouldn't go that far." Angel scooted off the chair and held out her hand to pull him up. He took it, but didn't use her as leverage. He just held it, not letting go. Her heart did a little skip.

"You stayin' for breakfast?" she addressed both her guests.

Aiden leaned down to brush dust from his jeans. The movement of his back and shoulder muscles under his shirt, was some of the best choreography she'd ever seen. *Mercy me.*

"Sugar, you'd better pick up your jaw before some critter takes it as an invite."

Aiden's stomach growled loud enough to send a flash of fur scurrying into the hydrangeas. Angel snapped her mouth shut making Chelsea hoot with laughter.

"I'd say that's a yes from your man. Count me in, too. I'm gonna need some sustenance to get me through the day. Grey took the boys fishin', says he's gonna bring us back some dinner." She rolled her eyes and turned to lead them back into the kitchen. "He said that the last four times, too. I've learned to keep some store bought fish in the freezer."

It took Angel's vision a moment to adjust to the darker interior. The smell of bacon and eggs was overpowering and heavenly. Their entrance interrupted the girls who were talking about some boy at school being a goober. Sonny sat at the table scarfing down his breakfast, blond hair still pointing in all directions. He had his headphones on, listening to music from the phone sitting beside his plate.

"That looks good," Aiden practically yelled so he could penetrate the noise pumping into her son's eardrums. *Their son.*

"Oh, he can't hear you. You have to smack him on the back of the head if you want his attention," Jessica interrupted.

"Truth!" exclaimed Addy.

Angel let go of Aiden's hand to remove the monstrous muffs from Sonny's head. "I've told you a dozen times, no devices at the table."

Sonny grumbled, but turned off the music, putting the items on the kitchen counter. He glanced at his father briefly before returning to shoveling food into his mouth.

Harrison was born two minutes and twenty-three seconds ahead of his sister, bald as a bowling ball. When Angel found out he was a boy, she cried, thinking how his daddy had missed the birth of his son. Then Aidrena came with her shock of black hair. She cried some more because her little girl wouldn't be able to wrap him around her little finger. Turns out, she wrapped her granddaddy around it instead.

Now, as they all sat around the table together for the first time, she wanted to cry again because here he was, finally meeting his children. The excitement emanating from him charged the normally calm atmosphere. She could see the shock lingering, and a truckload of hurt at missing out all these years. What would he do when he found out that his father knew? Or when he discovered the real reason they had to leave?

She wouldn't think about that today. He would find out soon enough. Let him get over this surprise first and have some time with his kids.

"Have you eaten already, Addy?"

"Yup."

Angel turned to Aiden. "Could you please fetch some plates? Addy will show you where." He may as well make himself useful. Chelsea already had bacon and eggs in the pan since there were extra mouths to feed. Angel started on the coffee. It was all so domestic. It made her uneasy.

They still had a lot to sort out. She had a ball of doubt in her stomach that told her, sometimes love isn't enough. She wanted to regurgitate that ball to get rid of it. Maybe she'd just smother it in bacon and eggs.

Angel put three cups of coffee on the table just as Addy guided her father to sit between herself and Sonny. Addy looked happy as a clam, and Aiden had a goofy smile on his face. Darn, that was endearing.

Sonny looked like someone had just given him a cake made with salt instead of sugar. She wondered how much of a problem that was going to be. She'd have to talk with the children, soon.

"So, *Daddy* . . . do ya like cars?" Sonny's grimace turned to a scowl. Was he taking exception to his sister's use of the name, 'Daddy'? *Oh dear.*

"They're okay. Necessary, I suppose." *Oh dear.*

Aiden looked at his daughter with amusement when she gasped in mock outrage. "Okay? Necessary? You wound me!" Addy clutched her chest and slumped back in her chair. The girl needed to go to drama class.

"I take it you're a car enthusiast?"

Aiden carefully pierced a piece of bacon with his fork, piling egg on its back before placing it neatly on his tongue. Angel watched as he closed his lips around it and dragged it back out, cleaned of its contents. *Dayum.* She wished she were made of metal with a handle and four tines. She must be more desperate than she thought. Memories of kissing that mouth and other things it had done last night made her vision hazy for a second. His presence was making her desperate.

"Uh, is the pope a catholic?" Addy's girly chuckle was infectious. "Are you gonna come have a look at Granda's shop?" She spoke with food in her cheek. Angel tutted, shaking her head. Her daughter was so much like herself at that age.

"Yeah, I'd love to." Aiden looked smitten already as he grinned at his daughter. His face probably mirrored Angel's when she watched him. Angel hastily straightened her features.

"Sweet! We're convertin' the brakes on a '67 Chevelle. You can help us out."

"You know how to do that?" Aiden rested his knife and fork on the edge of his plate, twisting to scrutinize his daughter more closely.

"Oh yeah, I'm a useful sort to have around. The H's are helping me fix up a Hemi Cuda. You should come check it out. I might even let you come for a test run when she's ready."

"Are you old enough to be driving?"

"Pshaw. 'Course I am." Addy waved the question away.

"No, she's not." Sonny and Angel protested simultaneously.

"Well then, I'll take you up on that offer as long as you stay in the passenger seat. Maybe you could help me find a ride. I'm going to need one."

Angel's stomach flicked up to her throat, leaving a lump she couldn't budge. He said all the right things. It sounded like he was certain of a future here. But wherever Aiden was the brute was sure to follow. She had a feeling this little bubble of Aiden's was going to burst. The power his father held over him used to be crushing. Had it weakened enough for him to finally break free?

Angel began collecting all the empty plates, interrupting the continuing conversation. "We're leavin' in twenty minutes. Y'all better get cleaned up, or I leave without you." The kids scooted out of the room so fast she was surprised they didn't make a dust trail.

Aiden stood to help her. "No, don't you mind. I can take care of this."

"I want to help you. I helped make the mess."

"Yes, you certainly did, Stud." Chelsea looked up at him through her eyelashes, one eyebrow raised. "Let him help you, sweetie, he's got a lot of makin' up to do." Chelsea smiled sweetly at Aiden as she placed the coffee mugs on the bench top. "Thanks for breakfast. I'll catch y'all later. Have fun." She beamed at a stunned Aiden before sweeping out of the room.

"She's an interesting character. Where did you find her?"

"She's a God send. And, she found me." Angel put her head down, concentrating on her cleaning task. That wasn't her story to tell, and he wasn't ready for that yet, anyways.

Chapter Eight

Harvey's Auto Shop had expanded since he was here last. The original building now housed the front reception, staff room and a couple of offices overlooking a waiting area. Angel stayed behind as he and the kids moved through to the workshop located in a large warehouse to the back.

Walking into the large space was like entering another world. Addy had a firm grip on Aiden's hand, pulling him along as he took in the place. There was enough room for four hoists, bays for another four vehicles under repair, and an extensive stock of tools and various parts. A large metal box in one corner completed the expanse. Aiden could see a car inside, taped up and ready for painting. Harrison aimed straight for the painting box and disappeared. His son was making it clear he didn't like Aiden's sudden appearance. *Be patient. Give it time.* He figured it would be the most natural reaction. So far, Addy had been excessively open and forgiving. He'd have to watch out for boys wanting to take advantage of her sweet nature.

The smell of grease and exhaust fumes coated every molecule of air. A country vibe kicked out from the radio diverting everyone's attention from the rumbling of engines and the metal on metal of tools doing their thing. This was not your regular auto shop. You could probably build a complete car here.

Aiden noted three classic muscle cars among the average vehicles in various stages of repair. He counted seven people working, including Angel's two uncles. He recognized Harvey's voice singing along where a Ford was on a hoist, the clinking of a socket wrench joining in the song. Four bays over, Harry fired questions at a set of legs poking out from beneath a Chrysler.

Addy yelled her good-mornings, receiving a chorus of replies as she stopped beside Harry. The men gave each other a nod and a slap on the shoulder. Aiden watched the disembodied legs jerk, working to slide the creeper along the floor, revealing a young man with a mop of curly black hair and mocha skin. His face cracked a wide smile when he laid eyes on Addy.

"Mornin', Sunshine. We workin' on the Chevelle today? Got the front disc kit in early this mornin'."

Aiden's eyes narrowed on the man. This guy had a thing for his daughter, clear as day.

Addy dropped her father's hand, jumping on the spot and clapping her hands together. "Awesome, let's do it!" She spun back to her dad. "Daddy, this is Tyler. He's one of Harvey's auto techs." Now smiling back at Tyler, she added, "Tyler, this is Aiden Thomas, my daddy."

Tyler stood and thrust an oil-slicked hand at Aiden, who was too busy watching his daughter's face to see if she had the same feelings for Tyler. He wanted to take her hand back and drag her away. She was fourteen years old. Way too young to be dating a guy old enough to have graduated high school. Way too young to be dating. Period.

Tyler jerked his hand back, grabbing a rag from his back pocket to clean up before offering it up again. "Sorry 'bout that. Nice to meet you, sir."

Sir. That jerked him out of his thoughts. He hated that title. "Call me Aiden," he suggested shaking the young man's hand, a little too forcefully, hurting his own injured hand in the process.

Tyler pulled his hand back and shook it out. "All right, sir. Aiden. Saw ya yesterday at the funeral. Addy knew who ya were straight away, but Miss Murphy was cryin' all over you, and we figured ya needed some space seeing as how—"

"Okay, Tyler. Shut your cake hole. There's far too much spewing out of it. Pull your socks up, Buck." Harry interrupted.

Tyler mimed zipping his lips and laid back down on the creeper, all but his legs disappearing once again.

Addy shook with silent laughter next to Aiden. "Don't mind him. He suffers from verbal diarrhea. Are you gonna help us install the disc brakes?" Eyelashes fluttered over hazel eyes, waiting for his answer.

"I have no idea what you're talking about, but I'll give it a go." She smiled her mother's smile and he melted a little more for this girl.

"Okay, but be careful of your hand. Grab some of those gloves over there." She pointed to a dispenser on the wall.

The next two hours involved learning about rotors, spindles, and single-piston versus twin-piston calipers. His hands ached from using them in ways he never had. The level of respect he had for Hank and his brothers, and for his daughter, skyrocketed. This was an art form in itself. Advanced puzzle building for mechanically inclined minds and strong bodies.

Addy struggled with the more stubborn bolts, Tyler eagerly jumping in to help each time. Aiden's instinct was to elbow him out the way, but he didn't have a clue what parts were what. He should've taken more interest in Hank's work when he was a kid, but he was too busy playing baseball and following Angel around, when he could sneak out. Until Hank bought him a camera. Then he followed her around with the camera hanging around his neck. Those photos must still be at Angel's place somewhere. He'd have to ask her about them. Only one photo survived his family's quick exit from Alabama, and it was still tucked safely away in his wallet.

Harvey sang the entire time, his Irish lilt lending something unusual to the country genre until Harry let out an ear-piercing whistle. "Anyone else Lee Marvin?" Harry's voice echoed in the large space.

"I am." Seven different voices yelled in reply. Harrison emerged from behind the glass doors, wearing overalls splattered in paint, a mask on his face and goggles on the top of his head. He made his way over to them removing equipment as he went.

"Lee Marvin? The actor?" Aiden asked Harry.

"Starvin', lad. Starvin'."

"Ah." Aiden nodded, the discomfort in his stomach making itself known now that he'd stopped working.

"Did Angel bring along the rest of the leftovers?" Harry was drying his hands with paper towel.

"Yes. We loaded up the fridge in the office this morning."

"Grand. Let's go eat." Harvey appeared behind him slapping him on the back, jolting his body forward two steps. He was going to need a chiropractor if he kept hanging around Harvey too long. Aiden joined the others in the line up to wash his hands as best as he could with the bandage, before lunch.

———

Angel could see Addy and her uncles crowded around the fridge, taking out various casserole dishes and heating them for the crew. The others sat around the long rectangular table gulping down cups of water from the bubbler, waiting for their plates to be filled.

The list of tasks she had to complete was out of hand. Adding hospital visits to the mix had completely thrown the routine. Angel wouldn't have spent that time anywhere else, but now she had invoices to enter, orders to fill, thank you cards to write, medical bills to find money for, and a lot of casserole dishes to wash and return.

She'd managed to sort through all the invoices from the hospital and had been on the phone to his insurance company for over an hour. They were going to have to sell Addy's Hemi Cuda. The papers sat in a pile on the corner of her desk, mocking her, taunting her with the repercussions of their presence. She did her best to ignore them while she caught up on some parts orders from the last two weeks.

Aiden filled her doorway. She didn't need to lift her head to know it was him. Her heart sped up, her entire body aware, practically swaying towards him. He smelled of grease and mechanic's soap. If she ignored him, maybe he would go away too.

"You ready for a break?"

No such luck. "You go on ahead. I'm just finishing up some things." *Please go away. I can't concentrate with you anywhere near me.*

Aiden moved so his thighs leaned against the front of the desk. She snuck a look under her eyelashes and got a straight view of his crotch covered in worn denim. Snapping her eyes back down, she typed some incomprehensible babble into her spreadsheet. Her fingers were slipping on the keys from her sudden outbreak of sweaty palms. She wiped them on her thighs and went back to punching in gibberish.

He didn't move.

The neat pile of medical bills on the corner of her desk did, however. They fluttered back into place as he let the corners drop. She flicked her eyes up to his face noting the frown marring his features. Locking her screen, she grabbed her coffee mug.

"Actually, I've a mouth on me. Let's eat." She marched out without waiting for his response.

Chapter Nine

Being in a crowd was safe. She flitted around the break room making sure everyone had what they needed, asking them about their families. She felt Aiden's eyes shadow her moves. They were practically glued to her, like a stray hair clinging to her shirt that she knew had been a part of her at some stage, but no longer belonged. She wanted to flick them off. Okay, no she didn't. She basked in his gaze wanting to douse herself in it for eternity.

A similar scene played out over the next few days. He would spend the morning working in the shop, and learning all about his children's talents and routines. He shifted between the mechanics with Addy and the cosmetic side of things with Sonny in the spray booth, even though Sonny kept kicking him out. That's becoming a problem.

Yeah, their babies were talented and hard workers. She was a proud mama. Aiden was a proud daddy, too. It gave her a thrill to watch him as he recalled his day, shaking his head in wonder, his eyes glazed over and a goofy smile on his face.

It wasn't helping her. Her stupid heart was letting him burrow inside again. An infection of loveitis spreading systemically. There was no cure. Not when he was insinuating himself so thoroughly into their lives, and his role as a father. He was willing to learn from his children, not pretend that he knew more than they did in some attempt at dominance and control. Not like his father. It was turning her to mush, dang it.

Every night Aiden stayed for dinner and then she drove him back to Saunders' place, dropping him off out front. She didn't dare get out of the car, and he never invited her up. He was being a gentleman, and she both appreciated and hated it.

Friday evening. Here they were back in her minivan. The drive from her place into town only took seven minutes. Seven minutes of breathing in his woodsy smell. Seven minutes of feeling the heat from his body beside her, his arm resting on the center console close to her side. Seven minutes of knowing that his eyes were fixed on her profile, and trailing up and down her body. She could feel it caressing her up and down every now and then, before fixing back on her face. She felt it in all those places he'd touched the last time she'd been up in Saunders' apartment. A molasses of sexual tension coated the air whenever they were alone . . . in a confined space. It should have been creepy, but Aiden was taking her in. She could feel him memorizing every detail of the changes he'd missed in her transition from girl to woman. Just . . . seeing her. Not asking for anything but to simply be.

That's all she wanted from him in return. Just to be here, for the kids of course.

God, no she didn't.

She wanted this man.

So much so that she started to doubt herself. Although she was grateful that he didn't pressure her for more, she wondered if he actually *didn't* want her anymore. If he saw changes he didn't like when he scanned her into his new memories. Was the sexual energy swirling around them conjured by her ravenous libido? Her eyes widened. *Sweet Jesus*, how embarrassing. She'd thrown herself at him because seeing him had reawakened her sexual mojo, and now the beast was alive and hungry, turning her into a pitiful mess of hormones. She was that girl at school who stalked the hot guy with unrequited lust.

She parked out the front of the hardware store, the headlights illuminating the display of ladders in the window.

She stared at those ladders.

Hard.

"Goodnight. I'll pick you up on Monday morning if you want. Maybe you can take the kids out to do something on your own. They need to get out of the shop and enjoy their summer break before it's over." *Before you leave to sort out your life.*

"Angel."

"Yeah." Maybe she needed a new ladder. That extendable one looked—handy.

He sighed. The rush of warm breath over her neck sent a shiver running across her skin. "Thanks for dinner and for the ride. Thanks for being a good mother and . . . just thanks for letting me spend time with them. They are so brilliant. I can't wrap my head around it. I know I keep saying that, but . . .

yeah." He dropped his head and shook it before raising it again. "I'll see you on Monday then." His voice descended from thankful to solemn.

She turned to look at him. His face, half lit by the reflection of the headlights, showed the shadow of his stubble and the glowing amber in his brown eyes. He was leaning close. Her breath stuttered as she took in his beauty. "Okay." Her hands were fixed on the steering wheel where they were safe. They wanted to be on his face and his neck and chest and . . . lower.

"Have a good weekend." His eyes glowed in the light as he smiled a sad smile.

She squeezed the steering wheel, and leaned slightly towards him. The click of the car door opening made her jolt back.

"Night, my Angel." His deep voice stroked over her name, setting her on fire. The closing of the door was like a loud slap across the face, and then he disappeared down the side alley.

"Night," she whispered.

She gave herself seven minutes to calm down before driving the deserted roads home.

———

Saturday. Cleaning day. She spent it stirring up a cloud of dust before swiping and sucking it all away again. Towels changed, beds stripped, load after load of washing. But still, there was far too much time for her thoughts to wander elsewhere. Specifically, to one sad, orange, 1970's sofa in an apartment above a hardware store. *Gah!* She was a hopeless case.

Her phone buzzed in her back pocket. She finished tucking in the sheet, and checked the screen.

Text from an unknown number.

Unknown: What are you doing tonight?

Angel: Who is this?

Unknown: The sad sack that's been hanging around you all week. AKA the father of your children.

Angel: Oh, the long-lost-love-of-my-life? That sad sack?

Shit. I mean dang. Why did I send that? There was no reply. She programmed him into her contacts. Her phone buzzed again after the long pause.

Aiden: Love of your life? Yes. I like the sound of that. You mind if I clutter up your sofa tonight?

A zing rushed through her at the prospect of seeing him again. Her palms started to sweat, making the phone slippery. Her breath fogged up the screen. She was holding it so close. It was official. She had no chance of resistance.

Angel: I happen to think you'd look mighty fine on my sofa.

Her finger hovered over the send button while her teeth abused her lips. She hit delete. If she took this step with him, it meant she trusted him to be here. For good. Not just for the kids, but for her, too.

Angel: That'd be fine. I'm dropping the kids at Chelsea's around 5:30. I'll pick you up on the way back.

She took another minute staring at the text before hitting send. *Oh, Lord. Here we go.*

Aiden: Brilliant.

Thank God, she'd cleaned the house. She checked the clock. Two hours to transform into a casual goddess and get the kids out the door. Easy as pie.

Aiden paced across the shag pile carpet, wearing a track from the door to the bathroom of the apartment. Every third round he checked the mirror again to make sure he didn't have any stray nose hairs, ear hairs or food in his teeth.

Hmm. He cupped a hand in front of his mouth huffing out and sucking the breath back in. Minty fresh.

He dropped his hand and spun around at the soft knock on the door. Power walking to the table, he collected his keys, wallet, a grocery bag, and a bunch of flowers.

He opened the door to find Angel, looking like—an Angel. Her pale skin against the dark fall of hair, and bright green eyes. It was a killer. She was goddamn gorgeous. How was she not already married? *Thank fuck for that.*

She had on a long, loose dress with some sort of colorful, swirly pattern, and thin straps holding it up. He followed the line of her body down to her painted toes in fancy flip-flops, and back up to her chest. No bra. His body grew taut and he gulped.

She waived a hand in front of his face. "Hello. Earth to Aiden."

He snapped his eyes back up, and shoved the flowers under her nose. "These are for you."

She took them with an amused smile. "Very beautiful and colorful. They match my dress. Thank you." He watched her transfixed. "You ready? Or have you changed your mind?" Her forehead creased.

"Ready!" he coughed.

She turned her back on him and seemed to float down the stairs as her dress fluttered around her legs. She had her hair piled on her head with loose pieces falling around her neck and face. He wanted to trace the curve of her spine, and bury his nose behind her ear.

He nearly mowed her down at the bottom of the staircase when she stopped abruptly. "I hope you still like Italian. I made a lasagna."

She had her back to him, looking at him over her shoulder. He dropped his chin and leaned in, breathing her subtle scent. "Delicious."

The pink blush coloring her chest and cheeks remained for the length of the journey home. He wished he could lick it. Good thing he had a grocery bag on his lap. *Calm down, man.*

The mouth-watering smell of tomato, basil and cheese accosted him as they walked in the door. "Like I said, delicious."

"I hope it tastes as good as it smells." Angel bent to take the dish out of the oven.

He held back a groan. "I'm sure it will." *I know for a fact that you taste as good, if not better than you smell.* She'd slap him if she knew what he was thinking. Then she'd toss him out on his ass. Horny teenage Aiden was making a resurgence. *He* wanted to slap himself.

Aiden emptied the contents of the bag to keep his hands and mind busy.

"You brought wine? And caramel toffee ice cream, popcorn, Gummy Bears and . . ." She picked up the DVD case he'd just put on the bench. ". . . Tim McGraw's Greatest Video Hits." Her lips puckered, holding in her laughter.

"I found it at the grocery store. It brought back some memories." He casually shrugged, putting the ice cream in the freezer. Fucking awesome memories. The first time she'd let him kiss her.

She served up the lasagna while he poured the wine. "Yeah, that was a great concert. I think he's touring again."

"Really? Would you go with me if I can get tickets?"

She looked at him across the table, a smile sneaking across her face. "I would love that." Her voice was so quiet he almost didn't hear her.

She tucked her chin to her chest, and cut into the steaming pasta. "Tell me about your life, Aiden. I want to know about all your adventures."

"Uh, I don't really know where to start. It's probably boring."

"Start with your favorite experience."

"Kids and animals."

Her eyebrows disappeared behind her hair. "Not the models?"

The hairs on the back of his neck rose. "Not the models. Kids and animals, definitely. If you need to stage a shoot, they're difficult to work with, but I don't really work that way. I aim to capture candid images. I want them to forget I'm there and just be natural." His vision blurred as his mind drifted through his memories. "Kids and animals are all natural, there's no filter, no pretense. Whatever is going on inside is displayed for all to see. I like doing portrait shots that expose real emotions, good and bad."

She was smiling at him, holding her glass of wine as he refocused on her face. "What about those beautiful landscape scenes you've done?"

"Yeah, it's interesting capturing the mood of a place that essentially stays put. It's the impact of the environment around that makes the difference. The changing light, the wearing weather, the interactions with the living things that use that space. I've got to get a feel for a place before I decide what angle to use."

"You love it."

"I suppose I do. It allows me to breathe, if that makes any sense. You could say, I haven't been in a good place—mentally, emotionally. It gave me a reason and a focus. The camera was my barrier, an excuse for escape, and a safe way to express myself.

"And, I'm doing all the talking. Very sneaky. You always knew how to make me spill my guts. Your turn. Tell me everything."

Angel chewed on her lips, spinning the stem of her wine glass. "Well, finding out I was pregnant was a shock. Obviously." She rolled her eyes. "The pregnancy was hard at first. The twins gave me double barrel morning sickness. Don't know why it's not called barf attacks, but anyways." He snickered and felt terrible all at once. "It got easier until I resembled the love child of a whale and a penguin, waddling along. I had to hold my stomach as I walked; they were so heavy. When I sat down, my stomach hit the chair before my ass. When you do things, you go big, that's for sure." She grinned at him. He wrapped his arms around his stomach, shoulders shaking, trying desperately not to choke on a mouthful of lasagna. He wished he could've seen her stomach round with his babies. She would've been gorgeous.

"Can I see photos?"

"Yeah, sure. Daddy took heaps. He couldn't get over how huge I was. There's an embarrassing number of baby photos, too. I kinda got carried away."

"That's a good thing, from my point of view."

She just nodded and grabbed the DVD, heading through to the library, steering him towards a spongy looking sofa in front of a dormant fireplace. She put the music on and brought out the old photo albums, flicking through to the soundtrack provided by Mr. McGraw.

He was right. She was stunning, even with the strained hint of a smile, and the dimmed light in her eyes. He'd done that to her. The knowledge cut him to the bone, causing a physical ache in his chest and a burn in his gut. She must have been so scared . . . she was only a baby herself. How did she manage school and motherhood? His brave, capable Angel. He didn't deserve her at all.

Aiden came to the pictures of his babies, his eyes stinging with emotion. They were so beautiful. Aidrena had weighed more at birth. What a surprise. It must have been all that hair where Harrison's was missing. He laughed at his son's frown in almost every photo where his baby girl was smiling wide, flashing her gums. Little personalities under development.

"I hate that I missed this," he murmured, flicking to the next page where a two-year-old Addy was caught throwing birthday cake at her brother. "Ha. She's a hellion."

Page after page of moments, frozen in time. First tooth lost, first day of school, birthdays, picnics, daytime naps, sporting events—years he missed. He smoothed a hand across the plastic covering each photo, his heart splayed on the pages. This is why he'd felt empty all these years. Back in this little town in Alabama, his heart and soul waited to revive him.

'It's Your Love' started playing, pulling him back in time to when he'd danced with Angel last. He tilted his face down watching as she sat leaning her head over his arm, waiting for him to turn another page of the past. She lifted her eyes to his. Gathered tears waited their turn to roll down her cheeks, and a wistful smile played upon her lips.

"Dance with me?" The words barely made it past the gravel in his throat. He placed the album beside him, and stood to offer his hand. The bandage was finally gone, exposing the healing cuts along his knuckles.

She smoothed a finger over the scars and took his hand, letting him pull her up. "I don't know how you've been workin' with those."

"Well, Tyler did all the hard stuff." The name came out harsh on his lips.

She giggled. "You don't like him much, huh?"

He slid his arms around her waist, having to bend a little because she was so petite. "He's after my baby. I don't care if he's a superhero, he's not good enough."

"Okay, Daddy. Put your shotgun away." She patted him on the chest, trailing her hands higher to circle his neck. The touch burned through his shirt, sending his heartbeat racing. There was no way she wouldn't hear it if she rested her head against him.

Angel let out a soft sigh and did just that. Her body molded against him felt unbelievable. His skin roared at him to remove all barriers between them. He squeezed his eyes shut, drawing in a deep breath through his nose. It made things worse. The smell of her hair, her skin . . . he wanted to surround himself in it.

It didn't matter what his body wanted, what his heart yearned for. Only she mattered. She had to be the one to move things forward. It was amazing that he was even here with her tonight. Nothing was going to happen until she was ready, because he had been the one to hurt her. Never mind that it wasn't his choice. That his mind had been tarnished, his memories blemished with doubt. He chose to stay away rather than grow some balls and come back searching for the truth . . . because he was scared that his father was right. That a couple of teenage kids weren't capable of that kind of love. Well, his father was absolutely full of shit.

The song changed to *'Please Remember Me'*. He pulled her in tighter.

"I played this song over and over, for years. It resonated with me. I was terrified you'd forget me, but I knew you would have moved on. How are you still single? Did you not start dating again?"

"Well, I didn't go and join a nunnery." Ouch. He deserved that. Fifteen years is a long time for a feisty, beautiful woman to be alone. Lord knows he hadn't been a saint.

"I didn't expect you to."

Angel lifted her head, looking him straight in the eye. "What about you? Didn't you ever find anyone that made you want to retire your suitcases?"

He shook his head, looking across the room behind her. "I never imagined getting married. I didn't want what my parents had."

She stiffened in his arms. The song continued in the background, McGraw talking of not being able to hurt his girl anymore. She stepped back, releasing his body from the warmth of hers. "It's getting late. I probably should get you home."

His stomach sank. *But, I'm already here.* "Okay. If that's what you want . . . Thank you for tonight."

She tried a smile that looked suspiciously like a grimace. He'd fucked things up. Again.

Bloody idiot.

Most. Awkward. Car ride, ever. His mind raced to think of how to fix this. He had to stop giving her so much space. She'd accepted him into her home to spend an evening alone. That had to mean she was ready for more. She'd let him hold her close, until his mouth had shot off again.

Things needed a push, and he knew just how to do it.

Chapter Ten

Monday

When Angel went to collect Aiden from town, he held a tray of vanilla raspberry muffins for everyone. Her favorite. He was bringing out the big guns to apologize for being an ass. He needed to do better than that, she thought, as she sat down at her desk where she found a note.

Dear Angel,

Every time you let me touch you I feel more alive than I have in years.
Thank you for the other night. You were beautiful with our babies in your belly.
Yours,
Aiden.

She folded it up and placed it in her pocket book, trying in vain not to let it affect her and failing. Yours. If only he was hers.

A knock at the office door interrupted her. "Come in."

"Hiya, Mama. Daddy wants to take us out so we can show him how the town's changed. Would it be okay if we took your car?" Addy's eyes had something shifty behind them. She was up to something.

"Yeah, I suppose. Is Sonny okay with that?"

"I told him he has to come. He's almost finished the paint job on the Charger, anyways."

"Mm. Okay. Don't let him scratch my baby."

"I will do the appropriate amount of backseat drivin', don't you worry." Addy flashed her pearlers, as she grabbed the keys, and ducked back out the door.

Aiden didn't make it back until closing time, telling her he'd dropped the kids off at home already. He looked sweaty and a bit muddied up. Alarm bells were clanging behind her eardrums.

"Did y'all go hikin' or somethin'?"

"Naw, we played a little ball at the park."

"Oh. Okay. Good, I'm glad they're havin' fun." She truly was. Guilt always gnawed at her every time they had holidays and she couldn't take them out. They actually enjoyed their time at the shop, but she didn't want them working their butts off. It was so strange to have someone else to share the parenting job with. She couldn't entirely relax, but she enjoyed the brief reprieve from all the responsibility, even for a short while. Maybe his timing wasn't all bad.

When she made it home, the note ended up in her drawer beside the bed so she could read it again . . . and again.

———

Tuesday

He stood waiting with a large paper bag, splotchy oil stains decorating its surface. Whatever was hidden in there was going to end up as thigh and ass glue. It smelled so dang divine, and when he opened the bag to reveal Danish pastries, she decided she hated him.

Another note awaited her.

Dear Angel,

I'm in awe of the woman you've become. After all the challenges you've faced, you've done a brilliant job with the kids and have given them a good life.
I wish I'd been here for you. You must've been so scared. You've taught me the true meaning of courage.
Thank you.
Love always,
Aiden.

The sweat from her palms stained the paper, as she folded and stashed it away to take home.

Why was he pursuing her when he didn't want forever? Her breaths raked in and out, she started to look around for that paper bag he'd brought in this morning.

His words were beautiful. On paper. He wasn't telling her what she wanted to hear. He was doing a darn good job of keeping her on edge and giving her mixed signals—keeping his distance, but dropping intimate notes, and buttering her up with sweet treats. Well, now she was just getting mad.

He'd taken her car and disappeared with the twins again. They must be exploring the national forest. There wasn't that much to see in town.

She snuck the last pastry for afternoon tea and asked her uncle, Harry, to pick him up for the rest of the week.

———

Wednesday

She worked from home, her courage all but drained. Seeing him every day, knowing he wouldn't commit to her, was like offering herself up to be gutted for everyone's entertainment. She needed a time out if she was going to put on a brave face in front of her family.

Her cell buzzed.

Aiden: Are you OK? Harry said you took the day off.

No, I'm not okay!

Angel: Fine, just working on some stuff from home.

Aiden: Do you need me to bring you anything? Lunch?

A time machine?

Angel: Naw. I'm enjoying the peace. Thanks anyways.

Aiden: OK. Take care. See you tomorrow?

Her mouth turned down, her chest deflating, thinking of another day spent in unrequited longing. Finally having him within reach, but knowing she had to let him slip through her fingers because she wouldn't take less than forever. Not with him. She deserved it all with the man she loved wholeheartedly. If she couldn't have it all with him, she didn't want half with anyone else.

Now she understood why her daddy never re-married.

She didn't bother replying.

All she managed to do was wallow, collapsing into bed completely wrecked by her overwrought emotions.

———

Thursday

He didn't come into the shop until the afternoon, holding a coffee machine under his arm. Her uncles cheered and slapped him on the back.

Hmph. She preferred sweet tea. Okay, except for that first cup of coffee in the morning. Dang.

Angel decided she might need an afternoon dose of java when she couldn't find her daddy's medical bills. "Dang it, where did they go?"

"Where did what go?" She refused to look at the owner of that voice.

Her fingers flicked through her filing cabinet. "None of your business."

Now she was being impolite. Chelsea would give her a high five. Angel let out a snicker at the thought. The sound died abruptly when her breathing jerked to a stop. She pulled out the stack of bills from a file marked 'Medical'. Red ink stamped boldly across each page announcing them as 'PAID'.

"What . . .?" She blinked several times, testing if her eyesight was failing her.

"You found them." She spun around to find Aiden crowding her door, each hand grasping a steaming mug. He walked in, placing the mugs on her desk, fixing his eyes on what she was holding.

She followed his line of vision and then trailed her eyes back to his, sucking in a breath at what she saw in their whiskey depths. Confession. "You did this?" She waved the papers at him, disbelief cloaking her features.

"Now . . ." He held both hands up, palms out. ". . . don't get mad. I wanted to do something for Hank. In no way was it a statement declaring you needed me to bail you out financially. I know you were on top of it, but I wanted to beat you to it. It was my final thank you to your daddy . . . Okay?" His hands remained aloft. She almost wanted to check if the Sheriff was on his way.

How could she be angry with the man? He had no idea that she actually couldn't have paid those bills. Not all at once. It really was a nice gesture. Angel didn't doubt his love for her daddy, or even his love for her. She felt it in every cell when he looked at her. His commitment was something else altogether.

She placed the bills back in the file and removed her shoulders from her earlobes, pulling out her chair to take a seat. "Thank you." She reached for the coffee. "And thanks for this, too." Her lips pursed to blow across the hot beverage, and the corners of her eyes crinkled in a smile.

He returned it, dropping his arms from the under-arrest position. "You're welcome," his smooth, deep voice travelled from her eardrums, down her neck, to the tips of her breasts. He grabbed his mug, winking at her before leaving. She watched his tight butt walk out her door. Lord, he did things to her. It was so unfair.

———

Friday

He brought his camera. Whatever he'd planned for today, she wasn't going to be a part of it. The kids were off to Harvey's place this afternoon, to watch some game on his big screen. She stayed in the office, hiding until after everyone had gone home, grateful for a bit of peace.

Angel opened her desk drawer to collect her keys, discovering a picture of herself when she was sixteen, and a Magnolia flower.

Her favorite.

A young Angel grinned back at her, green eyes flashing. So full of life, hope, and love. Love for the boy behind the lens.

She put the flower up to her nose, inhaling its sweet fragrance, and flipped the photo over. He had written 'My Angel. March, 2000.' Two months before he left.

Underneath, there was a stack of folded papers stuffed in an envelope. Most of them looked old and worn at the creases from frequent handling. She put the flower on the desk, and opened up the first one.

My Angel,
    It's been a week since m~~yffa~~ that bastard took me. I fucking hate him. (Sorry for swearing I'm just so goddamn pissed. Sorry again.)
    I miss you so ~~xxx~~ much. I'll never forget how you took me to heaven. I'll find my way back. I have to. Don't forget me.
    I love you.
    Aiden

Oh God. Reading his words, his frustration, just brought it all back. The horrible moment she'd lost him. Her hands shook as she folded the letter and put it back in the drawer along with the picture. Unable to swallow past the lump in her throat, she squeezed a hand around it trying to ease the pressure. Her nose was running, and water streamed from her eyes as she fumbled for a Kleenex. A soft knock at the door had her quickly wiping her eyes.

She heard Aiden curse under his breath. He looked horrified; his hands fisted against the doorframe. "Sorry. I didn't mean to upset you. I just . . . I wanted you to see. To see how I felt. How I still feel . . .. Ah shit, I've buggered it all up now, haven't I?"

"It's not that. I—I'm still a little raw, I guess. Your sudden return. Daddy's death. It's a lot to take in, and I don't really know what it is you're wantin' from me."

He dropped his hands and moved around the desk to stand beside her. "I know this must be hard. It's hard for me to grasp, too—losing Hank and finding you. By some miracle, you don't belong to some other lucky bastard, and you're still here. My favorite person in my favorite place.

"The thing is, I want to grab onto life for the first time in forever." He held out his hands, clenching them as if grasping for something. "I see you, and my heart beats so hard I can hear it.

"I've had that picture and those letters all this time." He pointed towards the drawer. "You know I'm not much of a writer. But I couldn't talk to you . . . and I needed to get the words out." Aiden shoved his hands in his pockets. "I never stopped thinking of you. The last one I wrote was two days before I came back, before I decided to look up my old hometown. It was my final goodbye to you. I guess I couldn't say goodbye to you after all. I thought you were a dream, but you're more real than anything. I love you. There's no changing it, or taking it back. I'll always feel this way." He seared her with the heat of his gaze. "I need you Angel, but I don't want to pressure you. I would take just living in the same town as you if that's all you'll give me, but I want more. I want it all, and I have to be a father to our kids."

He *needed* her, *loved* her. She was shaking, struggling to catch her breath.

"I was hoping you'd let me cook dinner for my family tonight? Let me make it up to you. Please?"

He stood before her looking so sincere and so . . . scared. His hands were in his pockets, shoulders bunched, eyes pleading. Angel's defenses were officially obliterated.

She could have sworn she heard her daddy in her mind. *"You're meant to be with him, Lass. The two A's. Just like my Helena and me. The two H's. He's the other half of your pair."*

Her daddy always did know what to say in any situation to make the insurmountable seem passable.

Her body relaxed. "Okay." She shrugged like it was no biggie, when really it was a monumental moment. At this stage, Angel would take anything he was willing to offer, and he was offering everything. A hundred tons of doubt lifted from her chest, affording Angel her first untethered breath since he left.

"Okay? Is that just an answer to the dinner or to everything?" He reached out a shaky hand, tilting her face up, searching for the truth. She gave him a wobbly smile, as off balance as he appeared to be.

He moved his hands to cover her collarbones, his gaze still trying to burrow inside her head and heart.

"Everything," she whispered. His thumbs started to stroke her skin with a feather light touch. His lids, thick with deep brown lashes, dropped lower as he zoned in on her lips. Her mouth dried up. She licked her lips and tried to swallow.

"Would it be all right if I kissed you, now?" *Yes. No . . . Yes.*

She managed to nod and the corners of his mouth tilted up in approval and triumph. His lips' descent was painstakingly slow.

Oh, dayum. He bent over her, crowding her into the chair and she loved it. Whoever invented kissing deserved an award. To want someone so much, you want to taste them, draw them into your body . . . it was a magical thing. Her whole being was dedicated to processing the feel of every part where they touched and tasted. His tantalizing smell and the slick, wet sounds of their mouths merging. She lifted her hands not knowing where to touch first. They decided for her when they landed on his hard stomach, the ebb and flow of muscle moving with passion.

He broke the kiss to whisper in her ear. "Sit up on the desk, Angel."

The heat of his breath, and the vibration of his voice shot tingles straight to her core. She felt her muscles clench, her body getting wet, preparing to welcome him inside. Her blood was burning through her, the desire for him overwhelming.

"God. Tell me I can have you. Please Angel, I'm dying here." His mouth took hers again before she could respond.

His hands skimmed up her thighs, lifting her skirt as they went. The desk felt cool under the back of her legs and bottom as she scooted back on its surface. Aiden widened her legs so he could fit between them, while latching his mouth back onto her neck. His hands gripped her ass, dipping into her panties to reach skin. She had to lean back on her hands to brace against his onslaught. The man was hungry, and that was just fine with her. No complaints. *Nuh uh.*

"Tell me. Yes or no?"

"Yes."

He growled and continued feasting. She whimpered when his mouth kissed down her chest, hands undoing buttons as he went. The stubble on his face grazed the sensitive skin of her breasts where they spilled over her bra. She felt swollen. Everywhere was throbbing. He pulled the lacy cups down, exposing her for a second, before replacing lace with his palms, and tongue. He'd found the off switch for her brain. Apparently, her nipples had more power than she realized.

"Put your arms around me and hold on." His deep voice confused her. *What is Barry White doing here?* She couldn't grasp the meaning of the words. One hand travelled past her belly button, burrowing into her panties, fingers stroking through her wet heat. She jerked up her arms flying through the air to wrap around his shoulders. *Oh, 'hold on'. Right. Gotcha.*

"Ah," she gasped as he thrust two fingers into her core.

"Fuck, you're so wet, and bloody beautiful when you're at my mercy." He pumped his fingers curling them up towards the front. "I dream about you every night. Dirty, filthy dreams about the things I want to do to you. About being the one to see your eyes the first time you open them every morning. Christ, Angel. I have it bad, you have no idea how excruciating it has been, having you within reach, and not being able to devour you." His words filtered through her mindless haze, but she was unable to respond, totally in his control. And she wanted more of it.

His fingers slipped in and out, gathering her juices, and rolling over the tight bundle of nerves every few strokes. Her fingers dug into his back, hanging on for dear life as her muscles gripped and released. Pressure built until she was strung so tightly she thought she might snap. His mouth was licking and sucking at her neck, her breasts, behind her ears. Their chests heaved in unison. He sucked in her ear lobe at the same time that he pinched her clit. She finally did snap, her legs kicking out, head thrown back, abs pulsing with the waves of pleasure tumbling over her. She heard herself crying out in relief, and then the sound of a plastic wrapper.

Suddenly, hands were pulling her forward until she straddled hard thighs. She felt her panties disappear and his shaft nudge her entrance before his hands gripped her waist, slamming her down onto him.

Aiden's groan was long and loud. She opened her eyes, only just realizing they'd been shut the entire time. She sucked in a breath at the hot look he was giving her. He was . . . feral. It enhanced her excitement to new levels knowing that she'd reduced Aiden to an animal. A naughty grin took over her face and she took control, moving her body over his. The office chair moved along the floor until it hit the wall behind her desk. She moved her feet with it, not caring. Only focused on the glazed look she was putting in Aiden's eyes, and the sensations they were creating between them.

He slid his hands up her back, pressing her body to his. Somewhere along the way, he'd removed his shirt. Hallelujah, because the feel of her breasts rubbing on his chest was ah-maz-ing. She'd never felt more carnal in her life.

"Fuck . . . Angel, I'm going . . . to come." He slammed his mouth down on hers, as his body jerked, emptying his release. She kept moving, leaning her pelvis forward to rub more firmly against him, drawing out his pleasure and sending her body crashing through ecstasy again.

Their harsh breaths mingled as they pressed their foreheads together, looking each other in the eye. With sweat-slicked bodies still joined intimately, they kissed again, more languidly this time.

"I love you."

"I love you, too." She stroked a palm down his chest. "I'm trying to decide if I should be pissed you had a condom, or impressed at your hopefulness."

"I'm impressed you said 'pissed'."

She smacked him on his abs. "I also say ass, but that's as daring as my vocabulary gets."

His hands squeezed her rear. "Say it again."

"Only if you show me yours." Her eyebrows raised expectantly.

"If you insist, but you'll need to stand up, and I'm not sure if I'm ready to let you go yet."

She rolled her eyes and eased off him. He was still semi erect, the used condom looking a little sad now that the fun was over. Her legs felt like jelly, so she leaned back against the desk, straightening out her clothes, as he stood, turning to reveal two very nice, firm, butt cheeks. She couldn't resist giving him a playful slap, the sound echoing in the room. "Nice ass. Make yourself presentable so I can take you home and you can feed me."

"Yes ma'am. Can I feed off you later?" His face was full of lascivious anticipation as he sorted out the condom, and pulled up his boxers and jeans.

"Nope. Not under the same roof as our kids." He laughed. It even sounded ridiculous to her ears. She looked around for her panties without success. "I think we should talk to them about what's happening between us. Give them fair warnin' before we go performing any PDA's and confusing or shocking them. Where are my panties?" She asked from under the desk, the sound of her voice suppressed by her posture.

His face turned thoughtful. He reached behind the monitor, grabbed the scrap of torn lace, and handed it back to her. "You're right," he nodded. "This is why you're such a good mama. You put them first. I respect that. A lot."

There was a sadness in his smile. She imagined he would respect that. With parents like his, concern for his needs was never high on their list of priorities. She would never do that to her children, and Aiden wouldn't either. They needed to sit down and have a family discussion. Soon. Because she wanted her family under the same roof.

Chapter Eleven

"Would you come with me a minute before I start the dinner?" Aiden asked as he was putting the ingredients for their meal in the fridge.

"Where are we goin'?" She had an adorable little wrinkle right between her eyebrows, her mouth in a pout that made him want to bite her lips.

"Just out back."

"Out back? Are you expectin' me to wade through the jungle to climb our tree? 'Cause I haven't done that since before you left."

"I do expect you to wade through the jungle, but not to climb the tree." He grinned, taking her hand and pulling her through the back doors.

"Aiden. What are we doing? I'm tired, it's been a big week. I just want to relax and enjoy someone else's cookin' for a change."

"Be patient, all will be revealed in a few more steps around this clump of bushes, and . . ." He swung his arm out with a gameshow flourish.

She gasped, her hands flying up to cover her mouth. Big green eyes blinking back tears. He really hoped they were happy ones.

She took tentative steps forward, and placed her hand reverently on the wooden gazebo he and the kids had been making all week. It wasn't quite finished. The railings had to be completed and it needed a coat of paint, but he was pleased with it. They'd planted little magnolia trees on either side of the entry step.

"I remember you used to talk about having one of these out here when we were kids. Your favorite movie was The Sound of Music, and you thought it'd be fun to dance around a gazebo like Liesl Von Trapp. I wanted you to have a haven in your favorite place, near our special tree. Addy and Harrison were excellent apprentices. Those kids have skills. I'm impressed."

He stood behind her, watching her frozen form just touching one of the supports of the roof. Aiden shoved his hands deep in his pocket to stop from pulling her body back into his. He sensed she needed a moment. *Shit!* Maybe she didn't like it.

"Don—"

"I love it. Thank you. Thank you so much. Those kids are getting something awesome for Christmas." She turned her beautiful smile to him, lighting him up with its brilliance.

"I'm so glad you like it. Do I get something awesome for Christmas?"

"Your Christmas just came today. You got me." She smacked him on the chest, and wrapped her arms around his waist. "You can have a hug now as a thank you present."

"I'll take it." His arms tightened around her, his nose and lips buried in her hair. Best Christmas present ever.

————

Chelsea sat at the counter with Angel, watching Aiden chop some vegetables for a delicious Satay Beef. The muscles in his forearms moved under his skin. Angel enjoyed watching those muscles move as he did other things. The sizzling of the beef strips hitting the hot pan sent a cloud of steam and heat her way, jerking her out of her fantasies. The aroma of peanuts and coconut permeated the air, making her mouth water.

Aiden wore a T-shirt and jeans, and he looked so comfortable and at home in her kitchen that she had a hard time concentrating on Chelsea's conversation.

"Are we still going to the drive-in after the opening?" Addy sat at the table swiping the screen of her tablet. Playing some game, Angel guessed.

"Hell yeah, sweetie. After we worship your brother's greatness, we're gonna have us a little Thor action," Chelsea answered louder than ever.

"Captain America for me. I like 'em a little less cocky." Angel winked at Aiden, making him suck in a breath and discreetly adjust his stance. She smirked, feeling giddy with her power. "I hope you haven't seen it yet. Do you want to come?"

"I can't remember the last time I went to see a movie." His eyes were sad though his mouth wore a smile. "I didn't realize drive-ins still existed. Is it the same one we used to go to?"

"Yeah, the one and the same. They've gone digital now. I don't think they make movies the old way anymore, so they've had to go digital. The sound is through the radio now, instead of the old speakers."

"Can we fold down the seats in your van?" He sent her a wicked grin as he added the noodles and sauce, turning down the heat.

The sound of his cell ringing cut off her response.

———

Aiden's grin turned to a scowl as he looked at the screen. "Would you mind stirring that every now and then? It only needs another few minutes. I have to get this." Aiden smiled at Angel, smoothing his hand down her arm. If he didn't answer this damn phone it would only keep ringing.

Aiden swiped across the screen as he backed away from the kitchen. "Thomas."

"Aiden." The stern voice of his father burrowed into his brain. Instant headache.

"Sir. Is everything all right with Mother?"

Aiden moved through to the entrance hall for some privacy.

"Your mother is fine. Where are you? I expect you to visit for her birthday. We're having a dinner party. Senator Lyndon will be guest of honor."

Senator Lyndon will be guest of honor at his mother's birthday party. Typical. He'd bet his left testicle that the good senator would be bringing his nineteen-year-old daughter. He was almost certain she was gay, and absolutely certain she was too young for him.

"Sorry, but I won't be able to make it this year." The false apology scratched across his tongue.

His mother wouldn't even notice if he didn't show up. The annual event was a barely veiled excuse for his parents to parade their successful, bachelor son around the available, young daughters in their social sphere. His father liked to lament that his son didn't become a lawyer, although he fed off Aiden's celebrity status and the attention it attracted.

"Why not? What could be more important than your family?" Mr. Thomas' voice cracked like a whip.

Exactly. "I've just found out I'm a father, and I'm getting to know my children. That trumps any attempt to pimp me out to the socialites. *Sir.*"

Silence.

He hadn't spoken to his father with disrespect since he dropped out of pre-law. Back then, he could blame it on youthful insolence. Now, it was born from betrayal and distrust. No doubt, his father was shocked that he was suddenly a grandfather.

"How dare you speak to me in that tone. Why did you go back to that godforsaken place? I took you away for your own good. You get on a plane and get your ass home immediately."

No comment on the grandkids. *Fucking asshole.* "No. I am home." Aiden managed to keep his voice cool. He nearly punched his finger through the screen as he disconnected the call.

Sonofabitch.

He couldn't go back in until he'd calmed down. He never wanted his kids to look at him in fear.

On autopilot, he walked out the door, strolling back to the tire swing he'd reacquainted himself with recently. The rope and tire didn't look as old as he remembered. Hank had taken care of his grandkids. Aiden couldn't have asked for a better male influence in his children's lives than the Murphy brothers, Hank in particular. Addy and Harrison would surely be well equipped for life, and have a better sense of humor than he ever did.

Looking down the road, he saw the house where he grew up. The ghost of his past wrapped in a scabby clapboard cocoon, and bookended by two brick chimneys. His mother used to wait on the front porch for the school bus to spit him out, quickly ushering him into the house's belly. A half hour later, when she was satisfied she'd done her motherly duty, she'd promptly forgotten about him. He could then sneak out the house's backside. The process of digestion was an unsavory and painfully slow exercise, if Sir was home. Aiden shuddered at the memory.

His phone buzzed in his pocket. Nope, not happening. He turned that plastic trap off, grasping his phone so hard it cut into his palm. One of the beauties of being on location was a lack of cell reception. The threat of paternal contact lurked somewhere closer to civilization. This was the only location he wanted to be at right now, cell reception or not.

Aiden climbed on the tire and set it gently swinging, the rocking motion doing wonders to calm his frayed temper. Being back here was like hitting the refresh button on his feelings. His overwhelming love for Angel, the belonging he felt to this family, the grief he felt at knowing he'd never see Hank again, and the hatred he had for his father since the moment he physically dragged Aiden out of town – all these emotions rose to the surface.

Aiden took a deep slow breath of saturated air. He could smell the promise of a storm creeping over the scents of the garden, an appropriate scene for his mood.

"Everything okay?" Angel stood behind him, arms encircling her torso and concern written on her face. *God*, she was sweet.

He jumped back off the tire and pulled her in for a hug, needing to steep himself in her. She grounded him and lifted him up at the same time.

"It is now." He kissed her on top of her head and stepped back, but grabbed her hand. "Are you going to let me make an honest woman of you one day?" For the first time in forever, he saw a chance at happiness and he wanted it . . . badly. He wanted her, them, his family.

Angel narrowed her eyes, one cheek hollowed as she bit the inside. "Not if that's how you ask me."

She never failed to make him smile. He decided to play with her a little. "Will you let me move in with you first? I don't know how much longer I can wait. And, if you're a typical southern belle, you're going to want the big wedding with all the trimmings." He laughed as she punched his arm. Hard, dammit.

"Maybe a spare room. Down the hall. Way down the hall."

Aiden's grin was wicked. "More exercise for me then."

"No, you don't." She growled, slapping him on the chest. "Children, remember?"

How could he forget?

The grin dropped from his face, sending her into fits of laughter. Her joy gave him a natural high, no drugs required. Fifteen years of missing her. He could wait a little longer. Although with the taste of her still fresh in his mind, it was going to take a Herculean effort to stay away.

They walked back to the house. "What did Chelsea mean about worshipping Harrison's greatness?"

"Oh. The Mayor is officially opening an exhibition of art works from the students at the high school. Sonny's photos will be on display over at the Town Hall. His art teacher set it all up. I think you'll be impressed. He's got his daddy's talent."

Pride like he'd never felt before coursed through his body. "Harrison's into photography? I can't wait to see them."

"It starts at one. You can come for lunch first. I'll pick you up around eleven, if that's okay. Teenagers usually don't surface until midday on weekends." She squeezed his hand as they entered the kitchen once again.

Chelsea scrutinized Aiden's face, her eyes narrowed. "Everything all right, Snapper?"

"Snapper?"

She moved her hands pretending to take a photo. "Yeah, Mr. Photographer. Snapper." Chelsea punctuated the comment with a wink.

Aiden's physical reaction to her cheeky gesture was vastly different to Angel's earlier wink. No zing straight to his balls, just an embarrassed flush of his cheeks. As if he needed further proof that Angel owned him. No other woman would ever have the power Angel held over him.

"You wait 'til you see what your boy has done with a lens. He'll be schooling you in no time."

He knew what Chelsea was doing. Distracting him with a 'what's really important' reminder. She was obviously an important part of his family's lives. Aiden was thankful to have her at that moment. She was perceptive, knowing just what he needed to hear. When he met her, she was ready to do battle. Now he understood why. Her bestowal of his nickname was her acceptance. He'd take it, even if he had to be named after a fish.

"I seriously can't wait." Aiden's smile nearly broke his face.

Chapter Twelve

Angel didn't sleep well last night. After the build-up of tension all week, the encounter in her office only made it worse. She was ready to explode. Not the most conducive state for relaxation. Now, some ass decided that he'd wake up the birds with a lawnmower on a Saturday morning.

Bless his heart.

The muggy morning air clogged her nostrils, and made the feel of the sheets wrapped around her legs unbearable. She wrestled them off, sitting on the side of the bed to grab a Kleenex. The clock said it was 10:18 am.

Shit. Sugar. She was supposed to pick up Aiden. Her stomach grumbled. She scrubbed her hands over her face, yawning in protest at the rude awakening. She processed that the lawn mower sounded nearby. Gulping down water from her bottle, Angel went to the window, peeling back the curtain to look in the yard.

Sweet Baby Jesus and all that is holy. Water spilled down her chin when she pulled the bottle away after over filling her mouth. Her cheeks felt like she was collecting nuts for winter.

Aiden was shirtless and sweaty, pushing the mower. He stopped, turned down the engine, and disconnected the catcher to empty it into the compost. The muscles in his back and arms moved in symphony. She had a thing for back muscles. Gulping twice to empty her bursting cheeks, more water dripped down her chin, wetting her tank. She grabbed the neck of her shirt to wipe it off and pressed her chest and forehead to the window to get a better look.

Aiden reattached the catcher and turned up the choke. The engine revved louder, assaulting her ears. He turned and looked up at her window staring at her for what felt like an hour before waving and moving off again. She stepped back and took a much-needed breath. Obviously, she'd forgotten to breathe.

She needed to wash up and get presentable. She was awake now, that was for sure. Practically running to the bathroom, she screeched to a halt when she saw what greeted her in the mirror. Birds nest hair with a *'Something About Mary'* fringe—check. Puffy, red eyes—check. Sweaty sheen to her skin—check. Wet, see through tank top displaying bullet-point nipples—check.

Oh my freakin' God!

Her groan was loud enough to compete with the mower. Aiden wasn't the only one putting on a show. She ripped of her tank and shorts and jumped in the shower, not even waiting until it was warm enough. The temperature was soaring in that bathroom. She washed everything—twice, before slipping into denim cut-offs and a loose, off-the-shoulder top. She twisted her dark hair into a wet, messy bun on top of her head.

A door opened in the hallway as Angel walked passed, revealing a groggy Addy.

"Why is Lawnmower Man interrupting my beauty sleep?"

Angel managed a maniacal giggle in response, skipping down the stairs before Addy could ask her anything else. She arrived in the kitchen just as Aiden came to the back door all sweaty skin and lean muscle. Her eyes drank him in. The close up was even better.

His wicked grin said he'd enjoyed the view in the window earlier. She felt the flush in her cheeks, and down her neck. His gaze tracked the changing color before fixing on her eyes.

"Good morning. Sorry about the noise. The yard's been bugging me, and I wanted to get it done before the day was wasted. I figured ten o'clock was enough of a sleep-in."

"Well, thanks, but Addy's not too happy with you. How'd you get here, anyways?"

"Mr. Saunders. Tim, gave me a ride. It takes some getting used to, calling all the older folks by their first names now that I'm getting old myself."

"Yeah, you're positively ancient at thirty."

"You must be prehistoric at thirty-one."

She laughed. "Our kids tell me so. Therefore, it must be true."

"I'll have to discipline them for sassing their mother. You're more beautiful now than you've ever been."

"Why, thank you, kind sir." The upward curve of his lips reversed at her words.

What had she said? "Uh, you can wash up in the bathroom down the hall. Don't get dirt on my floors."

"No, Ma'am. I'll do my best not to." He smiled at her, but his eyes held a tension at odds with his joking words. He tipped an imaginary cowboy hat and grabbed his bag, taking off in the direction of the bathroom. She stood staring after him for a while, wondering what the heck just happened.

———

Sir.

He fucking hated that name. As if the bastard knew Aiden was thinking about him, the name Sir flashed on the screen of Aiden's phone, as it vibrated along the bathroom counter. He pressed 'ignore' and leaned his hands against the sink, staring himself down in the mirror. He needed to avoid all mirrors in the future. Damn things saw too much.

He looked down at the phone. Goddamn plastic shackle. Rectangular marionette string. He might have managed to forge a career for himself away from his parents' influence, but . . . however he looked at it, he was still at their beck and call.

He was petrified that he might be anything like his father. That he wouldn't be a good enough dad. This was all so new. Suddenly finding yourself a parent to teenagers isn't for the faint hearted. He was so lucky that they were amazing individuals. That they had an exceptional mother and extended family, but they were still young. Rebellion was almost a certainty. Now that his father knew about their existence, he'd want to get his hooks into them. Attach those fucking strings. He couldn't let that happen.

Aiden took his time in the shower. He let the warm water wash over him, his fears being sucked into the vortex of water draining at his feet. He needed to get control back. He had to grab the happiness and love that was here for the taking, with both hands. Angel loved him. He felt it and saw it every time she was near. She was scared. Of course she would be. She needed to protect her babies, as well as herself. But, he wasn't a threat to their children. He was going to show them he was worthy of their love and trust.

When he found Angel in the kitchen, he had a renewed sense of purpose. She was seated at the table having coffee and cereal. There was no sign of Addy or Harrison yet.

"Feel better?" Angel's green eyes seemed to sparkle.

"Much better. It's hot out." He winked, causing her cheeks to color. He loved doing that to her.

Harrison barged into the kitchen. "You cut the grass? I was going to do it today."

"Well, now you don't have to." Aiden was taken aback with the anger coming from a normally quiet Harrison.

Harrison eyed Aiden's duffle bag on the floor. "What, is he living here now?"

"Harrison! Don't be so rude. Your daddy needed to wash up after doing the yard work."

"It's okay, Angel." Aiden turned to his son. "No, I'm not moving in. Yet. I hope to, someday soon. When you're all ready to have me. I want to be here as part of the family. Is that a problem for you?"

"Yeah."

"Sonny!" She started to rise from her chair. Aiden held his palm out to stop her.

"It's okay. He's been the man of the house since your daddy fell ill, and he feels he needs to protect you. He doesn't trust me yet. He doesn't understand that stampeding bulls couldn't scare me away. Not this time."

"I was only a year older than you when I left here, Son. If I had known about you, I would've been here sooner, fought my demons harder. You don't understand the love a parent has for their child. Neither did I, until I laid eyes on you both. Hell, even before I saw you. As soon as your mama told me you existed, my heart just about jumped out of my chest. It's incomprehensible, the magnitude of it, until it happens to you. Well, I feel all that and more for your mama. The last thing I ever want to do is inflict that kind of pain on her, or you, ever again."

"If you want to cut the grass, I'll leave that job up to you. But I'll be here doing other things around the house, because that's what fathers do for their families."

"I'm looking forward to seeing your work on display today. If it's half as good as what you can do to a car, I'm sure it'll be amazing. If you don't want me there, I'll stay out of your way, but I'm still coming to support you. It's your call."

He held his ground as Harrison stared him down. It was like looking at a younger version of himself in that damn mirror again, only this time he saw strength and conviction. That was a credit to his mother. She'd done a bloody excellent job. Harrison was more man than he ever was at this age.

Harrison let out a pained sigh. "Fine. The grass is my job. Your job is to make Mama happy, and maybe . . . fix stuff. Don't screw it up." He grabbed a piece of bread and shoved it in his mouth, eyeballing his father one last time before disappearing up the stairs.

"That went well." Aiden forced out a laugh.

"Ya did good, Daddy." Angel appeared pleased that they'd made progress.

He thought they were in for an interesting afternoon.

———

Town Hall stood proudly truncating the main street. Its red brick clock tower perched high in the center, a useless appendage since it had been stuck on 3:17 for as long as Angel could remember. Nobody was too concerned about the time around here, anyways.

The mayor stood on the steps leading to the entrance, doing his spiel about the art exhibition. His shiny, bald head causing havoc with Aiden's photos. Harrison, Jessica, and four other art students stood evenly on each side of the mayor.

She watched Aiden work, listening to him grumbling about the position of the sun as he switched out various tinted discs on his lens, adding some plastic contraption that looked similar to the blinkers race horses wear. He was in his own world, completely at ease behind the camera. Always the artistic dreamer, experiencing life through a fifty millimeter was a safe place where his genius could blossom.

Aiden wasn't the only snap happy parent. Jessica's mother was making a spectacle of herself, pushing through the crowd to get the best shot on her cell phone. Jessica rolled her eyes and whispered something in Sonny's ear, making him smile in her direction. He turned his head a second later, and Jessica's trademark smirk changed into wistful longing as she continued watching him. Angel sighed. Was he really that oblivious or just not interested?

She watched her gorgeous boy standing legs apart, hands clasped behind his back, staring off into his own daydreams. How many times had she watched a young Aiden doing the same thing? She bet he was praying for a diversion so he could slip out unseen and leave everyone else to the hoopla.

He was so reserved but get him talking about photography and you couldn't shut him up. On the car ride into town, her two boys had been engrossed in a conversation about F-stops and exposure times. It was all gobbledygook to her, but clearly important stuff for their craft.

Her two boys.

In the car, Sonny had told his dad that his first camera had been the one Aiden left behind. The camera Angel's dad had bought Aiden for his fourteenth birthday. He fell silent at this revelation, rubbing his thumb across his brow and checking out the stitching on his jeans. If she weren't driving the car, she'd have given him a hug. She could see him struggling with all the emotions of being back here and realizing what he'd missed. What he would never get back.

Her uncles stood behind her whispering about the mayor loving the sound of his own voice and commenting on Aiden's prowess as a photographer.

"No doubt about it. Our Sonny is just like his da." Harry nudged Angel's shoulder. She hummed her agreeance.

The mayor moved to the entrance and cut the thick red tape with gaudy, oversized scissors. His manic expression showing how he loved whipping those things out at every opportunity. She wondered if he got them out to do his Christmas wrapping as well.

Addy, Aiden and Angel caught up to Sonny, and they all entered the exhibit together. She had her eyes firmly fixed on Aiden's face, waiting for his reaction to the photographs. She couldn't think of a more fitting tribute to her father. Harrison had put together some candid portraits of Hank Murphy, some with him, Addy, and his brothers working in the shop, and one shot of Angel sipping sweet tea while watching the sunset. She hadn't even known he was there. It's the mark of a good photographer to be able to blend into the background and work around the scene to get the best shots, Harrison had told her with authority.

Aiden froze beside her. His jaw fell open slightly, and his brows pulled together in anguish and amazement.

"He's captured Hank perfectly," Aiden rasped, as he stood transfixed at the first photo of her father with his head thrown back mid raucous laughter.

She studied the photo for the hundredth time. This particular photo had given her some peace after her father died, knowing that his lively soul wouldn't be trapped in a broken body any longer. She knew her Daddy was free and stirring them up in heaven.

The twins broke off to find their friends and look at the other works. Aiden moved slowly along the display, scrutinizing every detail of each photo. They moved along to the last photo, the portrait of her. His hand stretched out, his fingertips not quite touching her image, as if she were just out of his reach. She saw regret, yearning and absolute adoration on his face as his eyes roamed the scene captured before him.

Tears flooded her eyes. She couldn't stop them. She'd kept pushing him away, punishing him for something that wasn't his fault. He had never wanted to leave. He would have come back if he was ready for a life with her.

Angel could only imagine what his father had said to a young and vulnerable Aiden. Always beating him down, making him feel less than acceptable. She could see the love on his face plain as day. She started to believe that this time their love could be strong enough to keep them together. Aiden deserved a chance to prove himself. Angel deserved some happiness.

She wrapped her arm around his back tucking herself into his side, this time trying to give him comfort instead of drawing it from him. "What are you thinking?"

He turned and pulled her body into his, her cheek snug against his chest. "I think Harrison's talent is going to leave mine in his dust." His head bent so he could murmur in her ear. His breath tickled down her neck, extending its reach with shivery tingles down to her toes. "I think both our kids are incredible people. I think you're still the most beautiful girl I've ever seen . . . And, I think I never stopped loving you."

He tilted her face up, his eyes burnished gold and shining with the intensity of his emotions. "I love you, Angel. I'm never leaving you ever again. Never. I know you don't really believe me. Yet. I'll make you believe it."

"Okay. Firstly, girl, no. Woman, yes. Thank you. Secondly, I think I believe you. I love you too. Never stopped, if I'm honest. So, you're stayin' and that's that." She squeezed him around his middle, causing him to grunt. Angel giggled.

Aiden's eyes flared with lust. He took a deep breath and let it out slowly through his nose. She felt the telltale bulge behind his zipper against her stomach. "Do you think it would raise some eyebrows if I kissed you in here?"

"Definitely." She pecked him on the lips. "Better keep it kid friendly."

Angel stepped away from him, noting that most people were ignoring them. Aiden pulled her back against him with an arm around her waist. "If we're keeping it kid friendly, you'd better stay in front of me for the next few minutes."

"Down boy. Wait until the drive-in later."

He groaned. "You are not helping."

She didn't want to help. She wanted to drag him out of here and have a proper reunion without tears and information bombshells. Bad mother of the year.

Angel surveyed the room. Addy was standing in a group with her friends, waving her hands around while telling a story. Harrison was doing his best to ignore two girls who looked about twelve, doing their damnedest to become his shadows, while Jessica ribbed him about his newfound fame. Chelsea was standing with her husband, Grey, talking to the mayor. She caught Angel's eye and wagged her finger. Obviously, she had caught the exchange. Angel shrugged her shoulders and grinned.

She shuffled her feet until Aiden was turned away from the crowd, and grabbed his hand. "Come on, Sugar. You need to meet Chelsea's family and the mayor with his big scissors. Think about the scissors. Does that help?"

"I'd say that did the trick for sure." His sarcastic tone was not thankful at all.

"Excellent!" She beamed and dragged him across the room to the people that held more importance in his life than he realized.

Chapter Thirteen

The drive-in had certainly changed since he was here last. It now had two screens, and the old concession stand was gone, replaced by a restaurant. There weren't many drive-ins left, but this one was still popular as long as the weather held off. Pickups and SUVs were the vehicles of choice, with everybody piled in the back, getting comfortable. Angel parked her minivan facing away from the screen in their old spot right at the back, away from all the noise of the restaurant and the kids running to the toilet. The best place to be if you're after private time.

Aiden looked out the passenger window at the pickup next to them. Two young guys occupied the back with a bunch of blankets and their girlfriends sitting between their legs.

"Help me fold down the seats?" Angel interrupted his gawking.

"Sure thing." He got out, nearly bumping into Harrison as he emerged from the back.

"Can we go meet up with Jessica and Drew?" Addy bounced on the balls on her feet, clasping her hands together, begging her mother. *Funny girl.*

"Who's Drew?" Aiden asked

"Jessica's brother." Angel answered him without taking her eyes off her daughter. "Do you know where they're parked?"

"Yeah. We saw them three rows up."

"Okay. Hold your horses. I'll give you money for some snacks."

"Thanks, Mama."

"Here, let me." Aiden drew a couple of fifties out of his wallet and rounded the hood with Sonny behind him. He handed one note to each of the kids, both taking it without looking. Addy ran off yelling, "thanks," over her shoulder. Harrison nodded and stuffed it deep in his pocket, ambling off in the direction of his friends.

"Did you just give them fifty dollars? Each!" Angel's arms hung useless by her side, her eyes wide with disbelief.

"Yeah?" He expelled the word slowly, bracing for a lashing from her tongue. Hmm. Actually a tongue-lashing from Angel would be a superb idea. His eyes dropped to her open mouth, where he could glimpse the pink of her tongue.

"You buy a new boat when your other one gets wet?"

He watched her mouth move, licking his lips. *Hang on. Did she just say wet?* "Huh?"

"You've got more money than sense. Why'd you give 'em so much?"

"I don't know. I guess they'll buy stuff for their friends, too."

"No good ever came out of spoiling children with material things. You've got to give them your time and your love, not a dime and fifty bucks!"

"I want them to have fun. Sorry, but I'm sure they're not going to turn into entitled brats overnight." He lowered his voice. "I'm working on more time and I already love them to bits."

Her eyes softened, her head tilted to the side in consideration. He stepped into her personal space, crowding her against the car. Raising his hand, he smoothed back some dark, silky strands of hair lifting in the breeze. She leaned into his hand. That was a good sign.

"You've looked after them all this time without me. I want to help, now. I want to look after all of you. My family."

"You have been." Her face lifted, deep green pools reflecting his image under the lights. He could easily fall in and get lost in her. Already was. "Just don't spoil us. I don't want them taking things for granted."

Aiden didn't move. His eyes roamed over her face. She closed her lids and lowered her face, shutting off his perusal. She'd said, "don't spoil *us*," and then put the focus back on their children. She was still guarding her heart from him. What more could he do to prove himself?

He smoothed a finger up her throat, lifting her chin as he went. "Open your eyes, my Angel."

She waited a few seconds before obeying his command. "There's my beautiful." Closing the gap between them, he rested his hands on her hips and his lips on hers. He spoke against the cushion of her mouth. "I am going to spoil you. You can take me for granted because I'm not leaving. Nothing could drag me away ever again. You're all in here." He placed her hand against his chest. "I need to be with you to keep my heart beating. Now, it has two more reasons to keep pumping. Don't you understand how much I love you? I was completely smitten with you the moment we met, but now it's infinitely stronger. I've been a satellite without an orbit. Don't let me drift again. Capture me." He slid his hands behind her neck, rubbing his lips side to side across hers, teasing but not taking.

She stood up on her toes, pushing her lips against his. He wanted to sink into her mouth, but he let her lead. Let her make the leap to meet him halfway. When her tongue ventured out, licking along the seam of his lips, he wanted to beat his chest in victory. She loved him as fiercely as he loved her. He'd felt it in every small moment of surrender. Any time she let herself feel without thought barging in to ruin the party.

She let out a purr when their tongues met. He groaned in response, sliding his hands down her smooth shoulders and arms, drinking in her smell and her flavor. He gripped the back of her thighs when she raised her leg in an attempt to climb him. *Fuck, that's sexy as hell.* His Angel knew how to take him to heaven.

She jumped up squeezing both legs around his waist. He jolted his hips forward, trapping her between him and the minivan, and putting his erection squarely where he wanted it. Angel's labored breaths matched his, loud through their noses as they rubbed together. He needed to remember they were in a public place.

The sounds of tires crunching over gravel, people talking and adjusting their radios to the right channel, were distant and garbled. The pounding pulse in his ears, chest, and his cock, were on board with drowning everyone else out. Aiden squeezed the handfuls of flesh he had in the palms of his hands as they continued to taste each other without being thrown out for public indecency.

A car pulled up beside them revving its engine, music blaring from its stereo at vibrate your bones level. Angel pulled back, dropping her legs and giggling at the look of ecstasy on Aiden's face as her body slid down his. He pressed another quick, hard kiss on her lips to take in her joy.

"Let's get these seats laid down so we can get comfortable." Angel nodded as he moved back to the passenger side of the van.

The music died down. "Well, hi there, Sugar. Decided to come up for some air?" Aiden heard Chelsea's familiar drawl coming from the newly arrived vehicle.

Christ. That woman always seemed to know when it was the most inopportune moment to arrive. She must have cock-blocking radar or something. He leaned in through the car, watching the two women embrace. Chelsea's smirk greeted him over Angel's shoulder.

"Evening." He waved, the corners of his eyes tightening as she wiggled her fingers back at him. Still smirking. No doubt, she was aware that he had to get himself under control before being able to greet her properly.

He set about getting the seats lowered, and the blankets and pillows set up. The task brought back so many memories of doing the same in the back of Hank's truck—watching a movie with Angel while her cousins did the same in their fathers' trucks on either side. The three H's and Angel's two aunts lined up in their camping chairs to the rear of the cars, doling out the treats as requested. And assisting with toilet breaks for the younger ones.

The door across from him slid open, snapping him back to the present. Angel grabbed the other side of the blanket and helped him spread it out.

"Chelsea and Grey are having a date night. Her mama's taking care of the boys. I don't think we'll see much of them tonight." She smiled up at him.

Good. He didn't care what Chelsea was doing in the car next door. He only cared about being close to Angel. Alone.

They had brought a couple of chairs in case the kids wanted the back. But it didn't look like they'd be back anytime soon. He stretched to take them out at the same time Angel did. His eyes locked on hers and then travelled down to a sight just as enticing, a whole lot of cleavage on display. He couldn't hold in the groan. The problem in his pants was back with a vengeance. "I'll take these. The sooner we get these out, the sooner we can get cozied up for the movie." He punctuated his statement with a wiggle of his eyebrows.

She snorted and rolled her eyes. "You sayin' I'm not quick enough for you?"

"You definitely have some catching up to do." He backed away, resting the chairs against the van so he could adjust his jeans. This case of blue balls was becoming chronic. She had him so wound up.

Greyson and Chelsea were setting themselves up for the movie, too. Angel sat swinging her legs over the back bumper, as she waited for him to set up the chairs.

As soon as he'd finished Addy and Harrison returned. *Unbelievable.* He immediately felt bad for the thought when he saw what they were carrying. Chili cheese fries, hot wings, a bucket of popcorn and cans of Coke.

"Ooh, yum." Angel jumped down to grab the popcorn.

"Thanks kids," Aiden added as they put the rest in the back of the van.

"Would it be okay with y'all if we stayed at Jessica's tonight?"

"Sure thing, sweetheart. Mind your manners and y'all have fun." Angel spoke around a cheek full of popcorn.

"Hang on. Jessica's mother will be home, right?" Aiden stretched to his full height, hands on hips.

"Yes, Daddy. She's here now, with Drew and Jess."

"How old is Drew?"

Addy rolled her eyes. "He's sixteen."

"You staying in Jessica's room?"

"No. Snickers usually sleeps in her room while I bunk in with Drew." Aiden choked on his spit when he inhaled instead of swallowing. Addy pounded his back. "Geez, relax Daddy, I'm just yankin' your chain. Of course, I sleep in Jess's room. How else are we gonna talk all night?"

Angel and Chelsea cackled in harmony. Harrison rolled his eyes, a reluctant smile on his face, and Grey stood grinning, shaking his head.

"Bye Daddy, night Mama. Bye Aunt Chels, Grey."

They didn't waste any time digging into the greasy food, sharing with Chelsea and Grey while the previews played. Looks like they'd be having a double date. He tried to lock his disappointment away.

"This parenting caper a bit harder than you anticipated?" Grey asked, tossing his head to remove the long dark hair falling over one eye.

Aiden dragged his hand across the scruff on his chin. "Yeah. It's . . . challenging. I want to wrap them in cotton wool, but I've missed all those years where they'd tolerate that. How do you protect them and give them independence at the same time?"

"You teach them good judgement and then you trust them, while praying and crossing your fingers," Angel answered for Grey.

Chelsea nodded, reaching for more fries. "And if they breach that trust, you ground 'em, and make 'em scrub the toilets for a month."

"Pfft. *You* do not. Your boys are still babies who think you know everything."

"And I'm holding onto that with both hands for as long as I can before they start speakin' in 'grunt' and rolling their eyes."

"My boys won't treat their mother that way if they know what's good for them."

"Aw, sweetie, it does things to me when you get all protective." Chelsea leaned over and shoved a fry in Grey's mouth. He held it between his teeth, giving her a salacious smile before sucking it in.

Angel groaned, mumbling, "Get a room," under her breath.

Aiden cleared his throat. "So, how did you both meet?"

"I came through town . . ." Grey narrowed his eyes in thought. " . . . oh, about nine years ago. Yeah, nine years. Met Chels and left the next day with her still on my brain. Then I turn up in Massachusetts to start a new job in this fancy restaurant and there she was, working as a server. I bought a ticket in the lottery the next day 'cause I knew my luck had changed. When she finished college and came back here, I came too."

"You've been here a long time, then?" Aiden asked Chelsea.

"Fifteen years." Her blue eyes pierced his, transferring some sort of message he had no hope of decoding.

Aiden's brow creased, his mind pausing to shake off the confusion, and collect the next question. "You would've known Hank well."

Grey hummed in agreeance. "Hank and his brothers are good people. Old school, community minded types. They bring you into their fold if they deem you worthy. It's a privilege to know them. Hank was like a father to Chelsea because it was just her and her mom."

"And I was best friends with his little girl so he saw me all the time. He couldn't help but love me 'cause I'm irresistible like that." Her flippant statement shook off the intense moment from before.

"You're so modest, Chels." Angel threw a piece of popcorn at her friend.

Chelsea's eyes grew wide and her back went ramrod straight. "Shhhh." She held both arms straight out, palms down. "Thor has arrived. Everybody shut up and sit back in wonder."

"I'm trying hard not to take offence," Grey quipped.

"Don't you worry, sweetie. You might not be a superhero, but you're a God in bed."

Aiden sprayed the mouthful of coke he was trying to swallow, all over the gravel at his feet.

Angel slapped him on the back, shaking with laughter. "You'll learn to brace yourself anytime Chelsea speaks."

Aiden coughed and sputtered, trying to get his breath back as everyone settled in to watch the movie. It wasn't until half way through that he thought about that weird look from Chelsea. She said she'd been here fifteen years. That meant she arrived around the time he left. When Angel had been shattered. *Oh.* She'd been there to pick up his pieces. No wonder she was acting like Angel's guard dog. He had to respect anyone who wanted to protect her. Even if it meant from him.

————

Aiden pulled the van into Angel's driveway, putting it into park. He noticed a black Mercedes parked in the street out front. His gut almost dropped through his boots. Only one man he knew would rent such an extravagant ride. The interior light switched on as one shiny black door opened revealing Brenton Thomas. The bastard had caught up to him. *Showtime.*

Dressed in a black designer suit, blonde hair now mostly grey, he was still an imposing figure. Aiden just wasn't affected anymore. The key to severing his father's control over him could actually be to give no fucks. He didn't understand that until he had something real to care about.

Chelsea and Greyson pulled up behind them. Their headlights beaming through the rear of Angel's car. Chelsea opened her door at the same time as Aiden, and they both stood to watch the unwanted visitor storm towards Aiden.

I guess drinks and conversation are out.

His father's steps faltered when he spotted Chelsea.

"Well, hi there, *Daddy*. I'd say it's good to see you, but it's pretty goddamn awful. You need to crawl back to your society buddies, and leave us the hell alone."

Chapter Fourteen

Aiden's head whipped around, mouth agape at Chelsea's words. *What*?

She turned to look at Aiden, apology written all over her face. "Honey, I was going to tell you tonight. I'm sorry. I wanted to make sure you weren't slicker than owl shit, like this one. And that you were stayin'."

"Chelsea, always unpleasant to hear you. Still uncouth as always. Prettier than your mother, though, thanks to my contribution to your genes. I hope you're making use of what I gave you to support yourself. The good Lord knows you didn't get my brains."

What the fuck is going on?

"Hey! Watch your mouth, old man." Greyson joined in the fray.

"Praise Jesus for that one, otherwise I'd be dumb as dog shit," Chelsea quipped in reply to her father. Greyson barked out a short laugh at the reminder that his wife could hold her own.

Brenton's face turned red, his mouth set in a hard line and eyebrows drawn low and tight. "Aiden. Pack your things, you're leaving with me. We have an event to attend. I won't have you letting down your mother."

Chelsea crossed her arms over her chest, cocking her hip and raising her eyebrow at Aiden. Angel had moved to stand between the two cars, the headlights putting her on center stage. Aiden went to her, taking her hand and pulling her to stand with him directly in front of his father.

"No." He wanted to scream about how his mother had always let him down, but what was the point? His father would scoff, or argue. He had no clue about a child's needs. Aiden was a possession—a trophy. The shine was coming off. Tonight.

"I have a sister and you didn't tell me? You cheated on your wife. Does Mom know?" As soon as he'd said the words, everything became clear. His mother's disinterest in him. Their interactions as a family, all carefully planned for the watchful eyes of society, when behind closed doors they were strangers. His parents had done a deal. His mother would provide Sir with a legitimate heir and fill the role of supportive wife for the cameras, in exchange for a place high in the social order and a plump bank account.

Air squeezed in and out of the man's flared nostrils, Aiden was surprised he couldn't see steam coming from Sir's ears. Any minute now, the foot stomping would begin. "You don't get to judge me, you little shit. She's not your sister! You're choosing this tramp over your own family." His father stabbed a finger at Angel's face, coming dangerously close to making contact. "This is a mistake you'll regret, Boy."

Aiden angled himself between Angel and his father, grabbing a handful of the bastard's shirt and lifting. "Don't. You. Fucking. Dare. Insult her, or put any of your person anywhere near her again. Do you fucking hear me, you sorry sack of shit?" Each word hit the back of his clenched teeth and ricocheted inside his head, turning up the pressure.

He barely registered a soft touch on his lower back. He didn't want Angel's voice of reason to talk him down. He wanted to expel the anger that had been festering for so many years. He let it splinter him, targeting the fragments into the marionette now hanging from his fists.

The man's hands flailed over Aiden's hold, trying desperately to free himself. Aiden easily had six inches on his father, but they were eye level now.

"Let go of me!" His father's voice cracked with fear.

Stale whiskey breath gusted over Aiden's face, and his father's jelly stomach heaved in and out pushing against Aiden's chest. The idiot was driving drunk, sharing the roads Aiden had just been driving on with Angel in the car. He could feel the muscles straining in his neck as the pressure gauge hit the red. "You have zero power over me. How does it feel to be the helpless one?" He dropped his father, who stumbled back losing his footing and landing ass first on the grass.

"Do you really think you'll be happy here? A man like you, a celebrity used to travelling the world? Having critical acclaim heaped on you?"

"Hell, yes! I don't want any of that meaningless shit. All I need is here."

The older man frowned for a second before a cunning shadow crossed his face, his mouth twisting into a sneer. He struggled to his feet, brushing his hands together. "Did you tell her that you have another bastard child? That you've abandoned another pregnant girl since her."

The touch at Aiden's back disappeared with his father's verbal blow. He heard more than one strangled gasp followed by hurried footfalls. He wrenched his body around in time to see Angel yank the door open, with Chelsea hot on her heels.

"Angel!" Her name tore from his throat.

Greyson didn't move, mouth turned down in disapproval, his eyes were two shards of flint stabbing into Aiden. "Like father like son. Is that how it is, Aiden?"

Aiden just shook his head clenching his fists, turning away from his new friend. He heard the click of the lock as Grey joined the women inside the house.

"You lying sack of shit. You'll do anything, and say anything to win your case, won't you? It's fuckers like you who give lawyers a bad name."

"We were meant for bigger things than what this town could ever give us."

"Don't you fucking speak as if you and I have anything in common. There is no '*we*'." Aiden clenched his fists tighter, probably splitting open his wounds, but he didn't give two shits. "Give me your keys and get in the fucking car."

Brenton smiled in triumph. "That's the last time you speak to me with disrespect, Boy. Don't need that southern slut and her bastards to drag our name through their dirty motor oil. Let's go."

Aiden's fist snapped out before he even had time to think. He saw his father fall to the grass in slow motion through a field of vision stained with red Vaseline. His knees hit the grass, blood dripped from split knuckles. High pitched ringing set the soundtrack to his explosion of rage. In his mind, he saw his fists pummeling their bullseye, but rough hands pulled at his shoulders preventing him from completing his violent desires.

"Get out of here, both of you. Angel doesn't need your bad blood staining her lawn." Grey shoved Aiden, making him tumble back in a parody of his father. Grey stalked back to the house as if he was done taking out the trash.

Aiden's harsh breaths felt like saws cutting his chest open. He rested his forearms on bent knees and hung his head.

Fuck! He'd lost her again, through his own stupidity. Sir strikes again. He didn't even get the chance to explain. She wouldn't give it to him now, not after he lost his control.

Fuck! Fucking fucker. He glared at the lump of flesh curled in a ball, clutching at his eye.

"Pick yourself up and get in the car," he growled, snatching the keys off the grass and stomping to the driver's side of the Merc. He sat gripping the steering wheel, glaring through the windscreen. A minute later, his father slumped in the seat.

Aiden took off towards Saunders' Hardware. "You better listen carefully because I'm only going to say this once. You will leave here in the morning and never return. Stay the hell away from my family. I am no longer your son. My father died two weeks ago."

"I will organize for my things to be packed and removed. If you choose to interfere, the story of your infidelity and subsequent abandonment of your child will spread through the media like wildfire. I will ruin you. Do you understand?"

Silence.

Aiden glanced at the man beside him. His father sat seething, a look Aiden was familiar with, but the effect was lost with one eye swollen shut and the man's disheveled appearance.

"Nod if you understand me."

Brenton Thomas' head dipped. With that one gesture, he finally felt the puppet strings snap. He was free.

He'd never felt more lost.

———

Angel sat at the kitchen table, staring through the back windows at the magical flying, flickering light show. Her happy place alight and alive, while she was dying from a fatal wound to her heart.

She dug her fingers into the wooden seat of her chair, her trembling so out of control she feared she would tumble to the floor. Maybe she should just curl up on the floor, then she couldn't fall any further, physically at least.

Her lids scratched across her dry eyes, tear ducts too shocked and exhausted to work properly.

"It doesn't make sense." She jumped as Chelsea's voice intruded on her internal battle. "You saw how he was with those kids; he'd stop a bullet for them. If he does have another child maybe there's a good reason why he isn't with them."

"Y—" Angel's voice failed, just as useless as her tear ducts. She coughed. "You're defending him?"

"I would take his word over that Brenton Thomas' any day. I don't know my brother as well as you do, but I think I'm a pretty good judge of character. He didn't choose to abandon you, like my father did with my mother. C'mon, Ange, there's foul play wherever that man goes. You know that better than anyone."

Angel rocked back and forth in her chair, still staring outside. She felt a hand smoothing down her shoulder. "Do you want me to stay? I can send Grey home to the kids."

Angel shook her head, biting her lips. "Go home, I'll be fine." Her voice came out surprisingly strong.

Chelsea kissed the top of Angel's head, the echo of flip-flops against the tiles fading as she and Grey left.

On autopilot, Angel went through her nightly lockup and bedtime routine. Sliding under the cool sheets, she focused on the ceiling. The old house emitted its own noises as it settled for the night. This place was a comfort to her. She'd be okay, even when she was alone. She'd be okay. The mantra was set on repeat in her brain, circulating the nerve corridors. Not helping at all.

She'd lost him again.

His eyes had turned black, empty. His body turning into a weapon with the force of his rage. She didn't know who he was in that instant, and it scared her. How many women had he done this to? Was he more like his father than she thought? Capable of callous abandonment? They'd left together. He was probably half way to Chicago by now.

She thanked God that her kids weren't here to witness the atrocious behavior on display. Protecting them was her priority. How was she going to explain all this to them?

As the shock wore off, Angel curled into the fetal position and wept.

Chapter Fifteen

Aiden sat on an old chair in Saunders' apartment. His father's snores disrupted the peace, or lack of it. The dove with the olive branch wasn't going to be visiting his life unless Angel was holding it.

Thomas senior had passed out as Aiden dumped him face down on the sofa. He was *not* like his piece of shit father. Getting a girl pregnant and abandoning her. The man was a giant stain on any life that he touched. He questioned why his mother had stayed in the marriage, but he finally understood it was merely an arrangement.

Chelsea was his sister. That meant that he had nephews, and Grey was his brother-in-law. This was unbelievable.

His father had taken more than he could have imagined, all because he didn't want to damage his precious reputation, and thought of a person's value only in terms of what they could offer him.

Aiden took a swig of whiskey straight from the bottle he'd found in the back seat of the Mercedes. He wasn't going to get drunk. He just needed to take the edge off a little while he waited for the sack of shit to wake up. The car keys were in his other hand, just waiting to get his father out of his town.

The apartment door flew open, sending a loud crack into the room as it banged against the doorstop. Chelsea stomped in slamming her purse and keys on the table. "Is it true?" Her eyes drilled into him, daring him to lie.

"No." He twisted the bottle in slow circles on the table, staring as the amber liquid sloshed around.

"Well, what the hell, Snapper?"

He looked up at her confused face, examining it for any resemblance. The blond hair was a lighter shade than his, probably with a little chemical encouragement. The shape of her nose, yeah that was the same. Her eyes were a different color—but the same shape. How had he not seen it?

He looked back at the courage in a bottle, not wanting another drop, but drawing strength from its proximity. "Earlier in my career, when I was doing fashion shoots, there was one model who became infatuated with me. I didn't see it at the time. We dated casually for a couple of months before I ended it. She was . . . needy. That's not commitment phobia speaking. I was genuinely concerned for her mental health.

"She started to stalk me. Three months later, she barged into a shoot looking very pregnant, demanding marriage and financial support because she couldn't get work. I knew it wasn't mine straight away. My father made it all go away. I made sure she got the help she needed. End of story."

"Shit." Chelsea plonked herself in a chair. "How'd you know it wasn't yours?"

"I always wrap it . . . and I've had the snip. Didn't want to be a father after the stellar example I was shown." Aiden leaned back, tapping his fingers on the edge of the table.

Chelsea blinked a few times then cocked her eyebrow. "That reversible?"

"*Hmph.* Yeah. Do you think I'm ever going to need to reverse it?"

"I'm not the person to ask." She tipped her chin at the sofa. "What are ya gonna do with that?" She screwed her nose up as if there were a putrid smell in the air.

"Take him back to the airport as soon as he's awake and I've calmed down."

"Then what?"

"I'm collecting my stuff and I'm moving here for good. My kids need me, and Angel needs to see that I'm serious. I could use some help finding a place, and a car. You know anyone who could do that?"

"Uh huh. You're lookin' at her."

He nodded, just managing to turn the corners of his lips up for a second.

Chelsea placed her hands flat on the table, tracing the wood grain. "My mama moved us here two days before you left. I was a bit of a hell raiser, constantly in all sorts of trouble. The idea was that I would get to know my brother, have some family around me. Well, Sir Sack of Shit wouldn't have it. He tried to pay my mama off when she was pregnant, telling her to get rid of me, and then asking her not to put his name on the birth certificate."

"You know, he came here three months after you left. Did the same thing to Angel. Hank threw him out on his ass. Called him a Bowsie. I think that means he's a waste of space, or somethin'."

Aiden tightened his hands into fists. "I'd have called him worse."

"We drove past your house the day we arrived and spotted you further down, talking to a red head. We only saw her from the back, as she sat on the tire swing. Mama took me to our house and went into town to see Brenton Thomas. Well, you know how he reacted to our arrival. I felt responsible for the pain y'all had suffered for a year, until I grew up and put the blame on the real culprit.

"My first day at high school, I saw Angel and knew she had to be your girl. She was a wreck. It only got worse when she found out she was pregnant, and then to have that visit—."

"Anyways, he refused to tell us where you were and didn't come back. Hank found out where your father worked. He flew to Chicago and followed him home, demanding to see you. You must have been at a boarding school. Hank loved you. He was worried sick about you and his heartsick daughter. Then you decided to be a nomad with no address. So, there ya have it, our sad little tale."

"Fuck! I was there locked in my room. I didn't know he'd come."

That son of a bitch had tried to stop his grandchildren from being born, or having his name. Aiden wanted to maim him. He wanted to destroy his father, but that would only hurt the people Aiden loved. The innocent bystanders in his father's sick game of take and tarnish.

Chelsea gathered her stuff. "I'll leave you two alone. You let me know when you'll be back and I'll have a car and a place ready for you. Let Angel cool down a bit before you try talking to her. I don't think she'll want to see your face just yet. I'll work on her."

"Thanks, Chelsea."

"What are sisters for?" She gave him a warm smile and winked as she left.

———

Angel dug her gloved hands into the damp soil. The organic smell she associated with her happy place did little to calm her soul and mend her heart. Weed after weed flew through the air forming a pile of unwanted trash. Pity she couldn't weed out her life. She'd known the brute would be back. He'd never be able to stand for his son living in a Podunk town with a mechanic's daughter and their illegitimate children.

She had smelled manipulation when she saw the skeevy look cross Brenton's face, but Aiden didn't deny his father's accusation, and he hadn't mentioned another child. That's what hurt. She had been completely blindsided by that assh—brute, once again.

Her hands moved with more ferocity, the more her emotions churned. The weeds had no hope. She needed time to cool off before she confronted him. Now that she'd slept on it, or rather tossed and turned on it, she didn't believe that Aiden would have left them to go back with his father. She was certain that he loved his children. If there were another child out there, he would never have turned his back.

The twins would want to meet their sibling.

She tossed another unwanted invader on the mound of ill-fated greenery.

"Did ya spend the night cleanin' the house from top to bottom too? What's next? Cleaning out the garage?"

Angel kept her back turned, grunting as she threw another plant, narrowly missing Chelsea's feet. Chelsea moved to stand in Angel's peripheral vision. "Didn't see you in church this mornin'."

"Didn't feel up to being thankful."

"You still have a lot to be thankful for."

"I know that, Miss Righteous." Angel sank back on her haunches and slapped her palms on her thighs, spraying dirt across her lap. "I'm entitled to some anger after the shit that was pulled last night."

"Whoa, name callin' and swearin'. Ya might need to go back to bed and get out on the right side next time."

Angel's shoulders sagged as she forced out a breath. "Sorry, Chels."

"Honey, I understand. I was here, remember? If you need a punching bag, go ahead and take a shot, but we all know who needs the smack upside the head, and I think your man took care of that last night."

"Yeah, I've never seen him that angry before. If I wasn't so scared, I might have cheered him on. He has changed."

"You've changed too. You're tougher, and wiser to the world. If you had been subjected to living with that prick, you'd be just as ready to lose your shit around him." Chelsea sat cross-legged on the lawn beside Angel, apparently not caring that she was still wearing her Sunday best. "I went to see him last night. He took Dear Old Dad back to Saunders' to sleep it off." Angel bit down on her lips, looking into her friend's eyes, so much like her brother's. "He didn't do what his father said he did. The baby wasn't his. He had a crazy model stalking him, trying to trap him into forever."

Angel dropped her eyes to her lap, clasping her hands together, the gloves making it difficult to squeeze and twist her fingers. "Oh my God! That piece of sh—work!"

"Yep. Mama picked a super sperm donor. But hey, she got me, so she won in the end, right?"

Angel leapt to her feet, Chelsea moving a beat behind. "I have to go and talk to him." She threw her gloves on the weed mountain she'd created, and brushed off her shorts.

"Uh. Well, there's a slight problem with that. He's not here."

Angel's head jerked up. "What?"

"He dropped the pile of shit at the airport, and then caught a plane to sort out his affairs."

"Affairs?" Angel's eyes bulged, her shoulders hunching in recoil.

"No, no, no!" Chelsea's hands waved frantically in front of Angel's face. "He's going to tidy up the loose ends, collect his stuff, and move it all here."

Angel's body sagged, her legs buckling so she stumbled a step. Her friend huffed. "Good Lord, woman, you need to go back to bed. Or, maybe have some hard liquor." She slipped an arm around Angel's waist, leading her back into the house. "C'mon. I'm throwing you in the shower and sending you back to sleep. The twins can come to our place today. Rest up before he comes back. You two have some talkin' to do."

Chapter Sixteen

Aiden was back. For good. His permanent address was no longer a post box in New York, and he wasn't living off a suitcase with his meagre belongings. Angel had talked to the kids about their daddy moving in with them. She thought Sonny might still have an issue, but he just shrugged and asked why it wasn't done already. Addy squealed, clapping her hands in true teenage girl fashion. Chelsea had organized for his things from Chicago to be packed and delivered to the house. Two boxes and a rusty old bicycle had arrived yesterday.

Angel wasn't up to the task of collecting him from the airport. Things needed to be said, and it was best not to do it while behind the wheel of a vehicle late at night. Chelsea volunteered to pick him up from Montgomery, she was excited to hand him the keys to a new Jeep. Apparently, he was dead on his feet, anyways. He'd ended up falling asleep in the car and Chelsea had to shake him awake to get him inside.

Angel opened the door with the spare key that Chelsea had given her. Her gaze zeroed in on the bed. She could see tufts of golden hair sticking up from under the sheet. She closed the door gently behind her and moved around the bed, needing to see his face.

Aiden let out a groan and rolled to his back, kicking the sheet halfway down. He was still in his clothes, his shirt unbuttoned and rolled at the sleeves. A jacket lay over his pile of bags on the floor, next to his shoes.

Her eyes greedily took in the exposed skin at the neck of his shirt. He was a beautiful man. She always knew he would be. He looked so peaceful, reminding her of the boy she had fallen in love with. *Have I ever not loved this man?*

A tenderness rediscovered rose in a tide of warmth. Angel's fingers itched to stroke the stubble on his face. Resisting the urge, she looked away, searching for a place to wait for him. Turning her back, she tiptoed to an armchair in the corner by the foot of the bed.

She paused with her butt stuck out behind her, hands gripping the armrests, when she noticed sleepy brown eyes blinking in her direction. "Hey," she breathed.

"Hey." He sat up on the side of the bed, rubbing his eyes. "What time is it?" he asked, squinting at her.

"Just after nine." She moved to stand in front of him. "Are you okay?"

He reached his hand out to take one of hers. "Are you? Christ, Angel, I'm so sorry about what happened. I lost my shit.

Years of pent up anger and the shame I felt at not coming back came rushing out." He pushed his eyebrows together with a thumb and forefinger, trying to erase the memories. "Then to find out why he took me away, it was just too much. That he's such a self-centered motherfucker he's prepared to destroy so many lives so that his remains perfect for public consumption. He knew about my children!" He smacked a palm on his chest. "*My* children, and he kept them from me."

"Hey, hey. Calm down." She gripped his shoulders.

"He lied, about the other child." Anxiety colored Aiden's face.

"I know. I'm sorry I believed it even for a second. I know you wouldn't withhold information like that from me. Having that man at my house, it put me in a bad place, mentally. I was a scared, vulnerable teenager again. My insecurities got the better of me. I'm sorry. I wish you had stayed to talk to me." Her hands squeezed his tense muscles in an attempt to soothe. "It's all done now. He won't be back, right?"

Aiden grabbed her around the waist and buried his face between her breasts. "*Mhnu.*"

Her hands took hold of his head, easing it away an inch. "I didn't quite catch that, say again?"

"No." Eyelids drooped over bloodshot eyes, his obvious fatigue tugged at Angel's heart. ". . . Not if he knows what's good for him."

"I didn't want to leave you. I figured you wouldn't want to see me right then, and I had to make sure he got on that plane. Far away from you. I wanted everything sorted out so there'd be no mistaking my intention to live out my life right here with you, Harrison, and Addy." The grip on her middle tightened as if he needed to tether her to him. "Are you going to be okay with having me around permanently?"

Her chest cracked open with love for this man. He was everything that had been missing in her life, and more. She inhaled, drawing it out as long as she could.

———

Her eyes closed, cutting him off from being privy to her thoughts. The pause, while waiting for her answer, stretched and crackled like perished elastic. He was vibrating with trepidation and love. Aiden scanned Angel's face, her thick lashes brushed her damp cheeks. She seemed unsure, her teeth digging into her plump bottom lip. His uncertainty knotted, lodging in his throat.

"I—I can't think straight when you look at me like that." She wrinkled up her nose. It was adorable enough to deter any annoyance at her non-answer. He had to smile.

"Like what?"

"Like . . . with so much longing. Like I'm the freakin' sun or something."

He laughed. "Good analogy." She lit him on fire as nothing else could.

When she smiled, he pressed his mouth to hers, caressing gently. Her palms slid up his chest and looped around his neck, grabbing on. He pressed into her harder and slipped his tongue between her lips, hers coming out to meet it.

Aiden had missed her taste, her smell, sweet jasmine and . . . Angel. She moaned quietly, the noise overcome by their harsh breaths. His hands drifted through her hair, one grabbing hold while his other hand smoothed down her side, grazing her breast before finally resting on her hip.

Aiden pulled her forward onto his lap so she straddled him, while he rested back on the bed. The heat from having Angel's body flush with his front made him feel like an eager teenager again, thinking with his hormones. He needed to calm this down. They'd finally made it to a proper bed and he wanted to savor her, but not until she'd answered his question. He slowed the kiss down to light sweeps of his lips upon the cushion of hers, wrapping his arms around her back. Aiden needed to hold her close, believe that this was real.

"Are we going to be forever, Angel?"

She lifted her head, bracing her palms against his chest. "Are you asking me what I think you're asking me?"

"Hmm. As much as I'd like to, no. You're not ready for that yet. All I'm asking for is a chance to be yours, and for you to be mine. No barriers, no fears or insecurities getting in our way. Can we try to be us, 3.0?"

"Ha. Cute. I think I can decide for myself what I'm ready for. I happen to have a spare room with your name on it. Would you like to come home with me?"

"Yeah. I really would." Aiden turned his head and checked his surroundings for the first time. "Oh wait. I asked Chelsea to find a place for me to live. Where are we, anyway?"

"You are the first guest to stay at Thompson's B&B. I'm afraid they don't take permanent guests. Your checkout time is at ten o'clock, so you'd better get your sweet butt movin'."

"Yes, Ma'am."

She scrambled back to her feet, holding a hand out to him. "Let's go home."

He grabbed it firmly. The look in his eyes triumphant.

"Home is wherever you are."

Titles by J. M. Adele

Coming Home Series

Shattered Home
Remembering Home
Finding Home
Leaving Home (Coming 2019)
Coming Home (TBA)

Sensing Series

Sensing You
Convincing You (Coming Soon)
Indulging You (TBA)

Bloodlust Series

Ashes and Dust
Ember and Flame

Excerpt from

Finding Home

The gas pump buzzed and clicked loudly, filling the air with fumes as Angel filled the tank. Chelsea leaned casually against the car, watching people out of the corner of her eye. She noticed Vince Walker filling his Ford, amazed that he'd gotten so tall. He was three years younger than her, and had been a cocky freshman when he'd asked her out. Moving away for college seemed to roll time forward, like a runaway train, rather than the tedious ticking of hands on a clock.

She jiggled her leg, trying to shake off the gnawing feeling that she wouldn't be coming back here to live. It sank in further, the closer she got to catching her plane.

Fucking crazy talk.

She might've been running away when she arrived, dragging heavy shit with her, but somehow, arriving here had lightened the load and made it all seem bearable. If she lost her connection with these people and this town, she'd be lost. The nervous energy ramped up until she was tapping her heel a hundred miles an hour, ready to take off.

Her attention shifted to a man she'd never seen before, and her heart instantly picked up its rhythm.

"Who is that tall drink of water?" Chelsea locked her sights on the stranger entering the gas station.

"Where?"

"He just walked in to pay for his gas. Long, dark hair. Brooding good looks. Tight ass cheeks in Wranglers."

Angel's eyes popped wide. "Keep your voice down!"

"Ass cheeks!" From the back seat, Addy tested the words on her child-sized tongue. Judging by the huge smile on her cherubic face, she liked the way they sounded.

Angel groaned. "Don't say that word, sweetie. That's an adult word." Unamused, Angel sent Chelsea a glare as she finished at the pump. "Thanks, Chels. Daddy is going to pitch a fit. Thank you very much."

Chelsea winced, keeping her gaze on the man as he spoke with the attendant. "Sorry, sweetie. You should be proud, though. She's a smart little sponge, aren't ya, honey?" Chelsea waved through the window at the little girl, before addressing Angel again. "I'll make it up to you. The gas is on me."

As she sauntered off, she put an extra sway in her hips to make use of her boots and swishy skirt. What was the harm in letting her free spirit soar just a little? She had her mama's blessing, after all. And something about the dark stranger reeled her in like a magnet. Her effort was rewarded when the man turned, stopping in his tracks on spotting her.

She made it to the door as he reached forward to open it for her. "Why, thank you, stranger," she drawled as she brushed past him into the shop. "Haven't seen the likes of you 'round these parts before. Are you just passin' through?"

"That was the plan. I'm just on the lookout for somewhere to eat supper." His voice caressed over every nerve ending, making things tingle.

Chelsea hummed in delight, never one to hold back her thoughts. "You should come to the diner. Fill up that body before you leave. There's not much to look at in the next town, anyways. The view and the company are much nicer here."

"No doubt." His pale gray eyes devoured her from under heavy lids.

"If you'd like some company, the diner is half a mile down the road. I'll see you there in a bit." It wasn't a question. She knew he was keeping up with her perfectly by the way their bodies vibrated and swayed towards each other. Her mouth watered at the thought of watching him eat, and talk, and look at her the way he was doing now.

His voice followed behind as she moved towards the register. "What's your name, sugar?"

Looking over her shoulder, she smiled. When a man wants to know your name, he's intrigued, if not half sunk. "Chelsea. What's yours, sugar?"

"Greyson." His barely-there smile was the sexiest damn thing she'd ever seen.

Her eyes dropped to the straining material covering his chest and biceps, before rising to meet his stare again. Nope, not just the smile. The whole delicious package. Stupidly, she wanted to go deeper. Wanted to know what made him tick. Whether he had the soul to match the body. She doubted guys like that actually existed, and trying to find one was a pointless exercise for dumbass romantics.

"Likewise, Greyson. I'll be seeing you real soon."

She watched as he blew out a long breath, threw him a wink, and went to pay.

Damn, her stomach was full of dancing lightning bugs. Or maybe it was a glut of waving red flags. She'd never been this excited to spend time with a man. Lucky for her, both of them were leaving. She could still have a little fun before she left. She wasn't going to go too far. She didn't do that anymore.

Much.

———

Like the rest of town, Lucy's Diner was stuck in a time warp. They had the jukebox to prove it, complete with vinyl records. It had a nice homey feel to it, though—another thing she'd miss while she was gone.

The bell on the door jingled as it slapped shut behind her. An aromatic cocktail of grease and coffee hung on the air, assailing her senses, and triggering her hunger. Chelsea turned and waved to Angel as she drove off shaking her head. Her friend thought she was crazy, meeting a strange man who wasn't hanging around for long. She'd learned to be more selective and trust her instincts when it came to men, despite her impulsive tendencies. Unwilling to repeat the fatal mistake from her past.

Maybe she was crazy, but there was something about him . . . She wasn't completely irresponsible. The diner was her turf and it was safe. There'd be people here that would look out for her.

She had this under control.

Chelsea's blue gaze roamed the cracked red vinyl booths, until they landed on the deliciousness that was Greyson Stranger. She didn't know his last name, so Stranger it was, and that's how she wanted it to stay. This was just a short detour to let off some steam before she had to get back to the serious business of paying for her sins.

Her smile stretched wide as she watched him take her in, the heat in his eyes blazing. His long, dark hair hung over one eye, brushing the tops of his wide shoulders. He leaned back in the chair and rested his arms across the table in front of him, with a hint of a smile in greeting.

Slowly walking towards him, she kept eye contact, half because she wanted to make an entrance, and half because she couldn't look away.

"Is this seat taken?"

Greyson waved his hand across the booth as if to say, "Be my guest."

Chelsea slid into the seat and rested her chin in her hands, still staring at him.

"Hi."

"Hi." He smirked.

"You hungry?"

"Yeah. I've ordered a piece of pie and sweet tea. I didn't know if you were gonna show up, so I figured I'd . . . fill up my body . . ." He wiggled his fingers to put air quotes around his use of her phrase. ". . . before gettin' back on the road."

At the mention of his body, Chelsea's eyes dropped to his straining T-shirt again. It was hard not to look. The man was gorgeous. "Well, sugar, if I invite a man somewhere you can always guarantee I'll show up. A piece of pie and some sweet tea sounds mighty fine right about now."

The waitress appeared in time with Chelsea's declaration. "Hi sweetie, good to see you again. You having what he's having?" The older lady stood with pencil and pad poised, and a ready smile.

"Thanks, Doreen."

"Okay, hun." She bustled back behind the counter.

Chelsea turned back to her companion. "So, tell me about your first kiss?"

Greyson's mouth dropped open and he huffed out a laugh. "Excuse me?"

"First kiss. Come on. Spill."

"Mindy Lawson, second grade, on the swings. How about you?"

"Decker Turner, two years old, in the playpen." She grinned. "What did you think you'd grow up to be when you were a kid?"

"Superman . . . How 'bout you?"

"Lois Lane." She smirked, batting her lashes playfully.

A deep laugh rumbled out of him, sending tingles down her neck.

"Do I get to ask a question?" He raised a dark brow.

"Only if it's not personal."

"Your first kiss isn't personal?"

"No." She shrugged.

"So, I can't ask what your last name is?"

"Nope."

"Or your number?"

"Nooo." She shook her head, dramatically.

He sat up straight and scratched the stubble on his chin, one side of his mouth quirked. "Arrabbiata or Carbonara?"

"Ooh, good one. It depends on my mood. Arrabbiata, most of the time."

"Spicy . . . Nice." He leaned towards her, his eyes dipping to her lips for a second, before seeking her gaze again.

She put her hands on the table, mirroring him as she leaned forward. "Red or white wine?"

"Whatever goes with the dish."

"I like an adventurous man." The smile broke out on her face again.

"I'm on the biggest adventure of my life."

"Where ya headed?"

"Isn't that a personal question?" He raised a brow and moved his hand closer so their fingers touched.

"Touché. Yes, it is."

The clink of plates on the table broke the intensity between them.

Chelsea took in a desperate breath as they both leaned back. "Thanks, Doreen, you're a darlin'."

"You're welcome, sweetie. Enjoy!"

They each took a forkful of pie, and chewed as their eyes roamed over each other. The taste on her tongue was amazing. The country song playing on the jukebox barely registered over the sound of Grey's lips smacking together as he enjoyed his food. He made a low hum in his throat, and she let out a whimper. It was the most intense foreplay she'd ever experienced.

She couldn't help feeling sad at the thought that this couldn't go anywhere. It should have been a warning signal, when fleeting hook-ups were the only relationships she dared to entertain. The type she could control. Maybe it hadn't been wise, starting something with this man. It echoed of her past. Of a stupid decision that cost a life. She feared she was setting herself up for a painful experience, rather than the fun she'd hoped for.

Picking up her glass, she gulped down some cool, sweet tea, looking away from him for a beat.

"Feelin' a bit heated, sugar?" The amusement was obvious in his voice.

The glass thunked on the table as she put it down too forcefully. "I am. You wanna get out of here?"

"What's the hurry? Are you tired of me already?"

"Nope. It's just the opposite. I'm afraid I've bitten off more than I can chew, but like the greedy girl I am, I'd like to gorge myself some more."

She had lost her everlovin' mind.

His jaw tightened and he paused, his eyes flashing to her mouth. She watched that jaw loosen as he continued to chew and swallow slowly. His gaze drifted back to hers, and he picked up his drink, draining it in one long chug before pushing the glass away.

"You're a wild one . . . Tempting."

He sat so still with his eyes boring into hers, his face an intense mask. His eyebrows had dropped. He looked almost angry . . . or maybe frustrated. It did nothing to dispel the heat that gathered in her core. If anything, the hint of fire in his eyes set her desire for him at furnace level. She'd never experienced an attraction like this before, putting her at a distinct disadvantage. She needed to be the one in control, and she felt anything but.

"I need to get back on the road. If I don't get out of here now, I'm never going to leave," he muttered, before he stood. Reaching into his back pocket, he pulled out his wallet, and threw some green onto the table. His warm palm caressed her cheek, as his thumb drifted across her bottom lip. The touch set off all sorts of tingles, further awakening parts that had no business being excited in a 1950s diner.

Chelsea's heart thundered in her chest as he leaned down to place a soft kiss on her lips. The barely-there touch seared more than the hottest chili.

"The first kiss is always personal," he whispered in her ear, before walking out of her life.

For good.

She sat for the longest time, staring at where he'd been sitting, trying to calm the hell down. Wondering what the fuck had just happened, and why she suddenly felt so bereft. Like her carefully planned future now had a gaping hole she had no idea how to fill.

Acknowledgements

This work was such a long time in coming. It was my decision to go to a masterclass on writing at the Brisbane Writers Festival that finally prompted me to let go of my fears and go for it, so thank you to everyone involved with that festival.

A big thank you to the fabulous members of my writers group. You rock!

I have to thank R.E.S. Tidmore, author and beta reader extraordinaire, for the trousers! For being so supportive. For reminding me to have faith in myself and to keep going.

Big thanks to my editor, Eeva Lancaster, for popping my cherry! Also for putting up with my newbie incompetence and for sorting through the dozen versions I sent her.

Thanks to my boys, big and small, for putting up with my writerly distractions and for eating toasties and baked beans for dinner.

To my friends and extended family, apologies and thank you for your patience and understanding when I neglect you.

To you, the reader, this is all for you. Thank you from the bottom of my heart, for giving me a chance. I sincerely hope you liked the story. I would love to hear from you.

To the bloggers, thank you for reading, reviewing and promoting. You put in so many hours of hard work with very little reward, but you make such a huge difference.

THANK YOU!

Author's Note

I sincerely hope you enjoyed this book. Please consider leaving a review on your favorite retailer's site. It truly is the best way to let the author know how much you appreciated the escape for a little while. And it spurs us on to write faster!

If you'd like to know when I have a new release available, please sign up for my newsletter. You'll find the link on my website.

About the Author

Former nurse, reluctant romantic, and reading addict, J.M. Adele, is the author of paranormal and contemporary romance, and romantic suspense. After years of indulging in her addiction to reading, her own characters started to tell their stories. They were relentless, forcing her to put pen to paper and release them into the world.

On most days you can find her juggling authorhood with motherhood while carrying a book in one hand. When everyone else drifts off to dreamland she escapes into the worlds conjured by the characters in her head.

Follow J. M.

Links to my newsletter and my Facebook reader group can be found on my website.

www.jmadele.com

www.facebook.com/authorjmadele

@JMAdeleBooks

@j.m.adele